"You Know Good And Well You Brought Me Here To See How Fast You Could Get Me Upstairs."

"That wasn't my intention, but if you're willing, I'm not going to pretend I don't want you."

She exhaled slowly. "There was a time when I would have done anything you'd asked, to hold your attention. Those days are gone. I'm no starry-eyed teenager offering sex to keep you interested. Not that you ever had a clue."

"I was a fool."

"You were a kid. So was I."

"And now we're adults. Any suggestions as to where we go from here?"

"Derek, I never intended to come here for anything but dinner."

"Then forgive me for giving in to my primitive instincts and I'll forgive you for enjoying it."

"This is where I should sputter and protest that I didn't."

He smiled. "You were never one for lying."

Dear Reader,

Check out the hot hunks on the covers of this month's Desire books. These are our RED, WHITE AND BLUE heroes, and they sure are something, aren't they? These guys are red-blooded, white-knight, blue-collar types, and they're guaranteed to make the hot summer nights even *hotter!*

Next month, we have a new title from Diana Palmer that I know you'll all enjoy. It's called *Night of Love,* and as an extra bonus it's *also* August's *Man of the Month* title. Also coming up in August are titles from Dixie Browning, Lass Small, Linda Turner, Barbara McCauley and Cathie Linz. Don't miss a single one.

And I'm still waiting for answers to last month's questions. What exactly do you like in Desire? Is there anything we can do differently? Do more of? *Less* of? No answer is too outrageous!

So, until next month, enjoy! And don't forget to let me know how you feel.

Lucia Macro
Senior Editor

LESLIE DAVIS GUCCIONE
DEREK

SILHOUETTE *Desire*

Published by Silhouette Books New York

America's Publisher of Contemporary Romance

SILHOUETTE BOOKS
300 East 42nd St., New York, N.Y. 10017

DEREK

Copyright © 1993 by Leslie Davis Guccione

All rights reserved. Except for use in any review, the reproduction
or utilization of this work in whole or in part in any form by any
electronic, mechanical or other means, now known or hereafter
invented, including xerography, photocopying and recording, or in
any information storage or retrieval system, is forbidden without
the permission of the publisher, Silhouette Books, 300 E. 42nd St.,
New York, N.Y. 10017

ISBN: 0-373-05795-4

First Silhouette Books printing July 1993

All the characters in this book have no existence outside the
imagination of the author and have no relation whatsoever to
anyone bearing the same name or names. They are not even
distantly inspired by any individual known or unknown to the
author, and all incidents are pure invention.

® and ™:Trademarks used with authorization. Trademarks
indicated with ® are registered in the United States Patent and
Trademark Office, the Canada Trade Mark Office and in other
countries.

Printed in the U.S.A.

LESLIE DAVIS GUCCIONE

lives with her husband and three children in a state of semichaos in an historic sea captains' district south of Boston. When she's not at her typewriter, she's actively researching everything from sailboats to cranberry bogs. What free time she has is spent sailing and restoring her circa 1827 Cape Cod cottage. Her ideas for her books are based on the world around her—as she states, "Romance is right under your nose." She has also written under the name Leslie Davis.

One

Teak Brewster raised her coffee mug in salute. Above her a flock of Canada geese circled the boatyard, dipped their dark wings and honked as they headed off Cape Cod toward the Massachusetts mainland.

"Pleasant journey," the twenty-eight-year-old called. "Central Park's the big green patch when you get over Manhattan." Teak sighed as she conjured up New York: the park, the Upper West Side apartment she'd sublet to a Julliard student, even the steel and glass view from her Wall Street office.

Behind her, in one of the corrugated metal sheds, John Kempski, assistant yard mechanic, had finally taken up the drill after a twenty-minute argument over her instructions. He had acquiesced only after a muttered, "You sure ain't your old man."

"Few people are," was her only reply as she'd left him to his tools. One month on the job and she already yearned for the din of Midtown traffic and logical arguments with co-workers who respected her judgment.

She was tired of being looked over, tired of feeling defensive, tired of being *here* when she wanted to be *there*. The worst part, which she was loath to admit to anyone, was the fact that day after day, subtle as the pull was, a hundred small things reminded her how much she'd missed this old yard.

Bud had had dreams for each of his daughters that went well beyond the confines of the chain link fence and cattail marsh. Nevertheless, Brewster Boatyard was the source of the love, the security and not a little of the talent she knew she possessed.

She glanced over her mug at the salt water, the precariously piled lobster traps, and Greg Delano, the yard's jack-of-all-trades, who was currently in the forklift stacking barnacle-encrusted docks for the off-season. She wrinkled her nose at the sharp, familiar, low-tide, mud-flat, fishhead and diesel-fuel stink that played such havoc with her emotions. Bud Brewster hadn't raised his daughters for this, no, sir.

None of the Brewster daughters was meant to come back to Brewster Boatyard and none had planned to, especially not Teak. Teresa "Teak" Brewster, like the sisters who preceded her, had been raised to strive for better things, things that education, comfortable income and fortuitous marriages could provide. The Brewster girls were raised to aspire to the life-style much of Skerrystead took for granted.

Teak's aspiring days were behind her, however. Of the three sisters, only *she* had found success entirely on her own, but like the others, she had gladly put the boatyard behind her, with Bud's blessing. Yet here she was, silk blouses and designer suits traded for denim and flannel. She touched her newly trimmed hair, the final sacrifice to Skerrystead.

A gust of wind rattled the corrugated boat sheds and whipped sand and dirt into miniature tornados, which scurried across the yard's pavement. In flush times the space would have been bow-to-stern with handsome yawls, ketches and sloops, yachts of all descriptions pulled and propped on jacks for the off-season, which on Cape Cod stretched from fall into spring.

Times were tough, however. From Boston to New York and Chicago belts had been tightened, and tightened again. Many Skerrystead summer people had been forced to give up their pleasure boats and the expense of hauling, storing and maintaining them. Some families even gave up Skerrystead. The client list at Bud Brewster's boatyard had dwindled to half. The timing couldn't have been worse.

Teak shivered and started for the office, sipping her coffee and reminiscing as she went. Today she intended to finish the inventory. For all his Yankee frugality, Bud Brewster had acquiesced to her insistence on computerizing the operation. Her suggestion, years earlier, had only been to make his life simpler.

"Little did I know," she murmured as she crossed the yard.

The pavement turned to gravel as she approached the main building, which housed the business office, small warehouse and store. It was vernacular architecture at Skerrystead's most quaint: clapboards, wooden porch, mullioned display windows instead of plate glass on either side of the entrance. Brewster Boatyard, Ethan Brewster, Proprietor still hung from the signpost out front.

As she reached the porch, the sound of an engine made her turn. A sleek bottle green sports sedan jostled over the rutted entrance, skidded in the swirling sand and pulled to a stop next to the sign.

A blond male pushed open the door, got out, mug in hand. He shut the door with a swing of his hip as he drained the mug and tossed it into the car.

Teak stood stock-still. She recognized the body language before she recognized the face. His adolescent swagger had mellowed into a confident stride. The years hadn't thinned or darkened his hair. Wheat was still his natural shade. His lanky frame had filled out, or maybe it was the season. He was fully dressed. She remembered him in a ratty array of shorts and jeans topped by polo shirts or foul-weather jackets. He'd had great legs, and a reputation that made girls discuss him in hushed tones. Her heart raced as he approached. She could have been a Skerrystead teenager all over again.

Teak was partial to men in pinstripes and business shoes, preferably polished within a inch of their professional lives—the men and the shoes. The man striding toward her would have done justice to any piece of clothing, but what he did for his teal blue chamois shirt, beige sweater and ancient khakis slapped her to attention like the prevailing wind. Her reaction was as unexpected as the sudden honking of the departing geese. A warning bell sounded in her brain.

Derek Tate shoved his hand into his hair to keep it out of his eyes. He'd forgotten how the wind whistled between the boat sheds. Now it hit him squarely in the back, urging him toward the woman on the porch. Not that he needed urging.

There was something disconcerting about her, something vaguely familiar. He watched her long enough to decide he hadn't known her, didn't recognize her. Still there was something beyond the fact that women were the exception in working boatyards. This one seemed to be staring at him. There was little in her glance that signaled approval. His scalp tingled.

As he approached, she straightened her shoulders. She was nearly as tall as he with a posture that would have made a mother proud. Yet there was no arrogance or even self-consciousness in her stance. She stood comfortably next to the porch support and made no move to enter the salesroom or come down the steps.

Everything about her was fresh. When was the last time he'd seen anyone in brand new, stiff, indigo blue jeans? Her shirt was a tartan flannel with reds as deep as the flush across her cheekbones, so new, creases still ran from the shoulder seams down over her breasts to her belt. He had to fight the temptation to linger over those creases.

Instead he glanced to her complexion. He flattered himself with the thought that it was his arrival that might have put the color in her cheeks rather than five minutes in the brisk autumn wind.

Her dark hair was a mass of waves and curls that framed her face as it caught the light. The breeze mussed it and in a gesture identical to his, she put her hand into it to keep it off her face. If there'd been distance between them, Derek would have let his glance linger. He would have savored his physical response. This was not a bad way to start the morning.

He caught her eye and she sized him up with a furtive glance. Had he been staring?

"Good morning," she said.

"Morning." Over the sharp sea-salt and beach smell of low tide, he caught the suggestion of something far more pleasant. Cologne? Hair spray? She let him pass. He entered the building feeling oddly rude, but completely invigorated.

The Brewster Boatyard salesroom brought back a flood of memories, and Derek stood still long enough to soak them up. Fishing poles, life jackets, tide charts, deck chairs, flotation cushions... Enough nautical bric-a-brac to sink any of his old man's yawls still lay under the glass display case. It all smelled of varnish, and weather, and time. The floor sagged where the pine had been worn to low spots. Derek recognized the fellow at the counter, but neither of the men in the aisle glancing at labels on cans of marine varnish looked familiar.

"May I help you?"

The feminine voice so close to his ear shot along his spine. The husky timbre was as much of a surprise as her presence. He turned. She was sipping her coffee behind him. She had the damnedest eyes, dark as her hair, but wide open, curious. Amused! No, this was not a bad way to start the morning.

"Remarkable how little this place has changed over the years."

"Feel free to look around." She stepped past him.

"I came to see Bud Brewster, actually. Is he in the back room?"

"No." She turned. "That's the one thing that has changed. Bud died last summer. If you're looking for him, then I'm the one you want to see." She put out her hand. "I'm Teak Brewster."

"Teak?"

She nodded. "What may I do for you?"

He took her hand, warm as her voice. "I'm Derek Tate."

She smiled as if privy to a well-kept secret, one of *his* well-kept secrets. "Yes, I know."

Two

Teak shook his hand.

Derek furrowed his brow. "Have we met?"

"Overlapped would probably be more accurate. Occasionally in a past life."

"Bud Brewster's daughter. Pin-straight hair, nearly to your waist?"

"That was Molly."

"Beat-up old station wagon?"

"Dana had the car."

"I'm sorry. Embarrassed, really." He snapped his fingers. "Teak. Of course. You're the kid who used to varnish our brightwork."

"Varnish was my specialty. Mahogany, teak—"

"That's where you got the nickname?"

"Yes. I worked here weekends and summers, behind the counter, too."

Derek cocked his head and wagged his finger. "Didn't I scrape you and your skateboard off Bay Road one August? Broken wrist?"

"Sprain. And it was Harbor Street."

He chuckled as he looked at their clasped hands. "It seems to have healed."

Teak withdrew her hand. "Nicely, about fourteen years ago." The warmth of his touch was already creeping up her forearm as if she were still that moonstruck teenager. She turned for the office. "Did you want to see Pop about business?"

"Yes. I'm sorry he's gone. I hadn't heard. I haven't been part of Skerrystead for some time."

"Thank you. We lost him unexpectedly in August." The usual lump in her throat made her stop.

They reached the back room, where the Brewster ancient oak desk was a jumble of invoices, correspondence and marine supply catalogues. Next to it, however, on their own cabinet, a computer and printer buzzed as they spit out perforated sheets.

"I'll be damned. Bud Brewster was computerized?"

"Teak Brewster's computerized."

Derek lifted a page from the printer. "Inventory?"

She watched the sheet inch its way over his hand. "Down to the last tide chart and paintbrush."

"Your idea?"

"I forced it on him a few years ago, not that he made full use of these capabilities."

Derek arched his eyebrows. "This is all your doing?"

"Yup."

"I remember Bud Brewster as a great guy. Knew boats like the back of his hand." Derek looked at the computer.

"That he did." Small talk. Pleasant banter. Teak took another sip of her coffee and tried to make sense of her physical response. Gut-clutching, heart-leaping palpitations were not part of her normal routine.

"You're holding down the fort?" He held his glance a second more than was comfortable.

"Yes." She managed to stare right back. "We lost Pop in August. I took over in September." She was about to regale him with the details of the professional life she'd put on hold, her leave of absence from Wall Street. She wanted Derek Tate to know how far she'd risen, how successful she was, but something more than the lump in her throat made her hesitate. Skerrystead, and men like Derek who personified it, didn't matter anymore. Let him find out for himself, if he was interested.

That inner alarm sounded again, set off by old times and old concerns, maybe old fears if she was honest with herself. She looked out the window long enough to collect her thoughts and damned him for making her feel self-conscious in her own boatyard.

It was Derek who turned. "Quite a setup you've got here."

She tapped the label on the computer, which read Tate Electronics. "You make a good product, but we've got everything we need. If you're here on behalf of your firm or your computer systems, you're too late." When she looked at him this time, his eyes seemed to darken nearly to the blue of his shirt.

"Hell, do I still look like I'm in electronics?"

"Systems analysts and computer salesmen come in all disguises. Last I heard you were following in your father's footsteps."

"Tate Electronics and I parted company some time ago."

"I hadn't heard." Her surefire cure for a palpitating heart was putting the other guy on the defensive. "Amicably?" she asked with the frankest glance she could muster.

The question seemed to startle him. "I'll save that for another conversation."

"If you're not here hawking computers, sit down." Something in her wanted him to sit, to lean back and get comfortable. She wanted him to pay attention, the way he never had back when it was important, back when ten minutes worth of attention from Derek Tate would have kept her going for a week.

He stayed on his feet, however, and continued to watch the printout, furrowing those brows again. "I'm here on boatyard business. I'm relocating—back to Skerrystead—and I've got a twenty-three-foot Bristol that needs winter storage and some engine work. Frankly, I was counting on your father. Bud was always the best. I was hoping he would be here."

"The yard's in good hands."

"I'm sure it is. It's just—"

"Derek, Pop never did engine work. Manny Souza's the expert. He's right across the lot in the machine shop." She stopped. "You look doubtful."

"Do I?"

"Go over to the shop and take a look, if it'll make you feel better. Talk over the problem with Manny." She swung in her chair and glanced at the chart on the bulletin board behind her. "We'll store your boat in shed two."

"Hard sell."

Teak unconsciously straightened her back. "This is business, Derek. We've stored, maintained and repaired your family's boats as long as we've owned this yard. The Brewster tradition won't change."

"Here's to tradition." Derek shook her hand again. It gave him the excuse to look at her, to feel the warmth of her touch, to try to make sense of her enigmatic response to him. "It's late in the season to be lining this up. You have shed space still available?" Her fingers tightened over his. Just as quickly, she withdrew her grasp.

"We have the room."

"Economy's been rough on you, too?"

"We've tightened our belts just like everybody else. We're still hauling. Where's your boat?"

Teak Brewster seemed to change before his eyes. Like fog off the mud flats, something settled around them. The atmosphere cooled. Just as well. The last thing he needed was an attack of surging adrenaline in Bud Brewster's boatyard. "In my driveway. Out in Wellfleet."

"You? You're living in Wellfleet?"

"Ever since I left Tate Electronics. I'm a joiner—cabinetmaker, master carpentry." He waited for the usual response and wasn't disappointed. Surprise settled over her.

"Really. You're a carpenter?"

"Joinery goes a lot further."

"I wouldn't have thought..."

Derek waited, but she shrugged and turned her attention to the computer. The woman was clearly stunned, and just as clearly was choosing not to comment. Instead she busied herself with the printout. The buzz stopped and the hum sighed into silence as she turned off the machine. The room grew suddenly quiet. "That's quite a step from your family's electronics empire."

This time, he decided to give her facts. "A step in the right direction. I've had my own shop and studio on the side for four years. Push came to shove, and I had to choose." He paused. "You look amazed. Can't a Skerrystead kid make it on his own in the real world?"

Teak smiled. "Certainly, but are we defining an outpost nearly on the tip of Cape Cod as the real world?"

"As compared to a hole-in-the-wall office in a Skerrystead boatyard?"

"Touché." She tore the inventory sheets from the printer and began to fold them. "To a member of the Tate family, I suppose this *would* seem like small potatoes."

"I didn't mean that the way it sounded."

"Don't apologize. It's perfectly understandable. Let's get back to why you're here. We were talking about your need for storage space. Why Skerrystead?"

He hesitated. What was it about this woman that made him chose every word he uttered, and regret half of them? "There's a pull to this old town. My family's always been strictly summer people, June to September. The idea of staying during the off-season appeals to me."

"Skerrystead's no different from Wellfleet. It yanks the shutters closed on Labor Day. What would you do for clients?"

"Clients are no problem."

"How nice."

Derek regretted his curt reply. It was becoming obvious that clients might be Teak Brewster's number one problem. His first glance had told him Ethan Brewster's boat sheds were rattling with empty berths. The economy was probably playing havoc with the boatyard.

He shoved his hands in his pockets. "It's the weak economy that's got me thinking Skerrystead might work. Rents are down, and there's shop space available on Market Street. The old upholsterer's place is for rent, and it has a full workroom in the back with easy access through the rear parking lot."

A knock on the office door made her turn. A man about their age entered with an engine part and an oily rag. He thrust them at Teak. "Alternator. Ain't often I'm wrong. You're old man would have replaced it."

"Humor me, John, and check the battery," Teak replied. "Please."

"Seems to me I been humoring you since the day you took over."

Derek watched Teak flush. His body stirred as he caught the rapid rise and fall of her breasts. He glanced at the hollow of her throat as she glared at her mechanic. How could it be that he hadn't so much as recognized her when he'd entered the yard?

After a deep breath, she smiled tightly. "John, that's what bosses are for. Talk it over with Manny, if you doubt my judgment."

"I might just do that." He turned on his heel and left the building.

A man in his late fifties Derek recognized immediately appeared at the door. "Did I hear my name?"

"John's doubting my judgment. I told him to see you."

"Needs the chief mechanic's opinion, huh, not some squirt kid, got too big for her britches?"

Teak tapped her chest. "This squirt kid grew up to know enough to suspect the battery's not holding the charge, even when it appears the alternator's shot. Give it some attention, will you?"

"Waste of my time. John should know better."

"If he doesn't, the customer loses. Time's no problem."

Manny gestured at her. "Problem with you is you grew up too much like your old man."

"Why, Manny Souza, just an hour ago you were muttering that I couldn't hold a candle to him."

"Well, there's plenty you still don't know."

"I know a heck of a chief mechanic when I see one. Give John a hand. I don't want him making more sloppy mistakes."

Now the mechanic flushed. "Good. Don't any of you go taking me for granted."

"You'd never let me."

He grinned and turned. "Well, if it isn't one of Jud Tate's boys. Derek, isn't it?"

Derek shook his hand, "Right."

Manny nodded. "I remember. Been a long time."

"Yes."

The men eyed each other until Manny gestured at Teak again. "Watch out for this one, Derek. Bud Brewster wanted a thing done, he'd bark. Teak here's got a way of making you come round to her way of thinking before you know she's done it. Don't occur to you to argue till you're two days into doing it her way."

Derek smiled at Teak. "I'll take that to heart."

Three

———

Teak chose to ignore the recalcitrant mechanic's teasing. Ignoring Derek Tate's perusal was far more difficult. She let them talk.

"I'm too set in my ways to be adjusting to a new boss," Manny continued. "Especially one I spent years shooing out from underfoot. Where've you Tates been? You give up boats altogether or you using another yard?"

"We scattered. We still own the family place out on the Point, but my brother's living in New Jersey. After the divorce, my mother went back to Seattle. Dad's retired. He does his sailing in warm water, Bermuda, the islands. However, I'm about to cut a deal with your boss."

Manny winced at the term. "Let's hope it's got nothing to do with alternators and batteries."

"It might. I've got a twenty-three-foot Bristol out in Wellfleet in need of a good going-over before she's put to bed for the season."

"I'd like nothing better than tinkering with a Tate craft. Yard's not the same without one of some sort. Of course, the yard's not the same without Bud Brewster, either." He glanced quickly at Teak. "But you're not to worry. Junior here's got everything under control. Loved your boats, I did. I was the one overhauled your dad's Hinkley about ten years back. Forty footer?"

"Forty-two."

"She was a beauty. Kept that engine purring." He nodded at Derek. "My best to your father. I'll be happy to look over your Bristol, soon as she gets here." With that he disappeared into the showroom.

Derek grinned as Teak sighed. "I gather he's not crazy about working for a woman who knows her engines."

"It's only the incompetent ones I worry about."

"The other guy doesn't seem overly fond of you."

"John Kempski. I made him take down his calendar, and that was the beginning of the end."

"Let me guess. Sailboats draped bow to stern with nudes."

"Naked women leaning all over car engines."

"Looking at that calendar probably kept *his* carburetor going."

The timbre of Derek's voice was doing devilish things to Teak's spine—the base of her hairline, to be precise. She cleared her throat. "Then let him hang it in his own garage, not my workshop."

"Fair enough."

"Really? How refreshing."

They were interrupted again, this time by the showroom manager. "Greg's out there with the truck and the cruiser. Jack Reilly's *Impulse*."

Teak glanced at the bulletin board. "Shed three. Behind *Duck Tails*." The phone rang at the desk. "If you'll get it, I'll go see Greg." Teak turned to Derek. "Greg Delano does our hauling. Come on out and we'll make arrangements for your boat."

She was glad Manny had interrupted. She didn't want to listen to Derek regale her with the successes of an electronics heir who had the money and contacts to give up a career and play at carpentry simply because he couldn't get along with his old man.

Instead she concentrated on business and spent the walk to the truck doing mental math and quick calculations. "So you're going to set up shop in the upholsterer's store. Have you found a house to rent?''

"For now I'll use our family place on Breaker's Point. That ark sits empty most of the year. It's winterized, and it'll see me through till spring.''

"No lease to break in case Skerrystead doesn't suit?''

He gave her a studied look. "Skerrystead suits me just fine. I'll be moving in a few weeks, if all goes well.''

They reached the diesel truck and the cradled boat. Teak gestured at the shed, then the driver. In good times Bud Brewster would have paid Greg Delano a full salary, but Teak had been forced to cut it back. He was now free-lancing with his own cradle, which made his schedule tight.

Derek turned away and looked at the huge travel sling that sat idle at the edge of the pier. In good times dock men would operate it hour after hour, hauling boats from the water and transporting them to their winter berths.

Teak bridled at the need for the yard to look bustling. The old ache to make a good impression manifested itself in her forthcoming invitation.

"Want a look at the machine shop?''

"Sure.''

That tender spot at the top of her spine continued to tingle as Derek followed her across the pavement to the open work space. She focused on

John Kempski as he glanced up from his tools and gave them a cursory nod.

"Manny or John will overhaul your Bristol."

"I don't know that it needs a complete overhaul, but I do have a list of stuff I've let go." He acknowledged the partition in the barnlike space. "What's on the other side?"

"It's empty. Years ago the mussel men used to clean their catch on the other side. Pollution caught up with them. Nobody musseling full-time from here anymore."

They walked outside and she winced as Derek glanced around. "It looks as though you've lost more than the mussel men. How many berths are still empty?"

She bridled at giving an honest answer. "We've got enough room for yours, Derek."

"This late in the season."

"It's only the first of October." Silently she cursed the boatyard. She cursed Skerrystead and all her sweat-and-penny summers behind the counter. As a teenager, she'd had no business trailing after boys like Derek Tate. *Men* like Derek Tate were no better.

For all she knew he had a portfolio and a client list that read like the *Social Register*. Old resentments began to simmer. Old inadequacies rustled despite her successful years in Manhattan. This windblown hunk of hometown gorgeousness had no right to stroll back into her life and make what she'd accomplished evaporate as if she were a fourteen-year-old still facedown in the sand on Harbor Street.

Once out in the sunlight, Derek watched the sea breeze catch Teak's collar and ruffle her hair. He smiled at the thought of her rattling around the old boatyard persuading hotheads like John Kempski and grizzled mechanics like Manny Souza to come around to her way of thinking. Whatever her style, there was no doubt the woman could be very persuasive.

She was lost in thought and he nudged her. "I was observing, not criticizing."

"I'm used to criticism."

"It goes with the job, I suspect."

"One of the headaches. Between sailors giving up their yachts because of the economy, and my father's loyal employees steamed over being bossed by a female, I've got enough to last me till Christmas."

"Old salts don't take kindly to new ways, male or female."

"New ways are what'll keep us afloat." She pointed at Greg. "Let's arrange for your boat."

They discussed it with the driver as Derek pulled out a pocket calendar. He concluded his business regretfully, and Teak walked with him toward his car.

"It'll be good to be back," he said.

"Will you be fending for yourself in that ark of a house, as you call it?"

"I *fend* just fine."

"I'm sure you do. I was just wondering if you'll be needing any work done, cleaning help, winterizing, that kind of thing. If it gets to be too much for you, there are plenty of people in town looking for odd jobs."

"As a matter of fact, I could use some cleaning help, once in a while. Anybody in Skerrystead you recommend?"

"I'm sure I can come up with somebody."

The rhythm and sway of Teak's stride was a fascinating combination of business and femininity. Her personality was quicksilver, fresh as a sou'east breeze over the dunes. Maybe he was a fool to have come back. Then again, for once in his life, perhaps he'd found something to hold his interest.

Midmorning two weeks later Derek threw another log on the fire and rubbed his flannel sleeves. The Wellfleet chill was a promise of weather to come. He was looking forward to the move to Skerrystead. In the days since he'd sealed the boat delivery with a second handshake, he'd been unable to shake thoughts of Teresa Brewster.

The brunette boatyard owner couldn't have been further from his type. Skerrystead townies had never been more than summer romances. Nevertheless, Teak Brewster had picked up polish somewhere along the line and wore her confidence like an old sweater. She didn't quite approve of him, and he knew it.

He was used to women's overt reaction to his family name and connections. Until his abrupt career change he'd been linked to one for whom that life-style had been the glue that had held them together. The trouble with Teak Brewster was that it was impossible for him to devise a good first impression. There was far too much in his very public Skerrystead existence he'd have to live down.

Despite everything, even from Wellfleet it had taken the first week to shake constant thoughts of her, and the second to quell the urge to make the trip back and ask her to dinner.

There was something intriguing about her determination and the drive that did everything but ooze from her pores. The way she'd looked at him was part analysis, part disdain. God only knew what she'd recalled from his less-than-sterling adolescence. It had never occurred to him that by pulling into the Brewster Boatyard, he'd be exposing himself to the old hometown scrutiny.

He grabbed a mug of coffee and a jacket, and headed for the harbor. The familiar Portuguese lilt of his neighbor Maria Santos reached his ears as he closed the door. She was leaning over her fence, deep in conversation with the wife of a commercial fisherman. He let the familiar laments over wholesale fish prices and the local school board pass, and waved away an invitation to join in the conversation as it turned to hurricanes.

The off-season solitude enveloped him, and he hunkered into his jacket as a gust blew off the water. Time to move on. The signs were unmistakable. Vague discontent was constant. Bone-deep restlessness made concentration difficult. Always there was the feeling that he was outside looking in. His interest in the school board went only as far as the bite they took from his taxes. Commercial fishing didn't affect him unless a fresh catch wasn't available. Hurricanes were few and far between.

He felt as disconnected from Wellfleet as every other place he'd tried. The trendy isolation of the tip of Cape Cod was no more home than the fashionable suburban communities of his childhood, or the stylish condominium from his executive-on-the-rise days. He'd even tried the Tate Park Avenue cooperative apartment for six months. Nothing pulled at him; nothing beckoned. Nothing anchored him except his work, and for the time being the empty house in Skerrystead. Regardless of the disasters of his September-to-May existence, his summer memories were clear and good, if not always calm. It was time to go home to Skerrystead.

He thought again of Bud Brewster's daughter. *Teak.* Exotic, rare. Intriguing. It made Skerrystead all the more palatable. He grinned as he imagined Teak Brewster's confrontation with John Kempski over the calendar.

The deep rumble of an arriving truck made him turn, and the sun glinted off the windshield as the brakes moaned. The truck inched its way down the street. Derek waved and turned around, motioning in the direction of his cottage and the boat propped on jacks in the driveway.

The air brakes squeaked, and the truck and cradle lumbered past. As he reached his driveway, he shielded his eyes. The cab of the truck opened, and Teak Brewster jumped onto the pavement from behind the wheel. Her heavy cotton sweater came right down to her thighs, which were covered in well-worn denim. Pink socks peaked between cuffs and leather boat shoes. Her eyes were shining and she grinned, obviously enjoying his surprise. Pleasure began a slow dance from his scalp to his toes.

Four

Teak concentrated on Derek Tate's amazed expression as she slammed the cab door shut. He stood on the sidewalk surprised, amused and as disarmingly gorgeous as ever.

"Greg came up with another assignment," she said.

"Why does it surprise me that you can handle one of these things?"

"It shouldn't."

"There's no rush at this end. It could have waited for Greg."

She frowned. "Why?"

He shrugged. "I hope you didn't feel obligated to make the run just because we'd agreed on today."

"Even if you don't, I have a schedule to keep. I don't feel obligated, and it's all hydraulic." She wasn't about to admit that her hands were still sweating and her heart was lodged somewhere just south of her larynx. The twenty-three-foot Bristol sloop was clear of any obstacles and facing forward. She thanked heaven for the favor.

"Handsome boat, with the exception of the brightwork."

He turned suddenly. "Don't look too closely at the handrails."

Teak clucked an admonition. "Too late. I've already noticed the neglect. Some sailor you are." The wooden trim was faded to gray in places, dry and tired in others.

"Just never got to it, this year. It needs the old Brewster touch." He gazed at his boat. "Funny thing is I really did think about that kid at the boatyard who took such good care of the varnishing." He turned to her. "Teak Brewster, a master with steel wool and varnish. Who knew it would turn out to be you?"

She looked into the fathomless blue eyes. "Who knew?"

Her reply drifted between them. She watched him blink, felt his stare and tried to ignore the pinpoints of excitement. She should have waited and sent Greg.

Thirty minutes later, the boat was snugly in place in the cradle behind the cab. Derek motioned toward the cottage. "How about some lunch? Keep your energy up. It's a long haul back in that thing."

She laughed as she got out of the cab. "I don't even have to shift gears."

"Don't ruin the mystique. The thought of you manipulating that rig is fascinating."

So was the realization that he'd been thinking about her. "I'm glad you're so impressed. Maybe you could manage to have some of the attitude rub off at the boatyard."

"In these times, they probably think their jobs hang in the balance."

"I'm painfully aware of that, Derek, twenty-four hours a day." The sudden warmth of his hand at her back startled her.

"All the more reason to take a lunch break before you go back and face the music. Let's pick up some sandwiches at the bakery."

Unconsciously she moved into his arm. "All right, if it'll include a tour of your studio."

He arched an eyebrow. "You're interested in something?"

"I'm curious about your work. The heir apparent leaving his family's electronics empire is something out of the sixties. I'd like to see if you're any good."

Derek's reply was a penetrating look.

She touched his arm as sunlight caught his hair and brightened the crown. "Sorry. That was a weak stab at humor."

He laughed sardonically as they crossed the street. "Doesn't matter, my secret's safe. The shop's just tools and sawdust at the moment."

"Giving up Tate Electronics must have been a big step."

The edge returned to his voice. "Well thought out. It wasn't a whim."

"Some people thought so?" The pressure of his touch disappeared as he dropped his hand.

"Some people."

"Your father? I assume your departure was less than amiable?"

"You asked me that two weeks ago."

"I know. I've been waiting for an answer ever since."

"My departure was long overdue and barely missed."

Teak walked next to him in silence. After half a block she said, "You're not going to elaborate?"

"No need. It's done."

"Long overdue, maybe. Barely missed? There's too much bitterness in your voice for me to swallow that one."

"I thought you were here to haul a boat."

"I'm curious about why its owner's coming back to town."

They reached the bakery and he immediately started a conversation with the clerk. They ordered sandwiches, and she would have loved nothing better than a thoughtful, "So, tell me about the last ten years," while the clerk made them. Derek Tate, however, didn't seem the least bit anxious to offer any more information than was necessary. If she had any sense she would follow his lead and keep to the impersonal business at hand.

She inhaled the aroma as he bought a loaf of Portuguese bread, then walked with him through town. When they reached his door, she waited and a moment later he ushered her into his two-room cottage.

He got the reaction he'd expected. She stood in a white-washed room centered by the fireplace and not much else. A threadbare overstuffed couch faced the glowing hearth. Wicker chairs framed a tired drop-leaf table. The only thing of value, a Tate Electronics stereo system, sat under the window, and books packed a series of shelves.

"Cozy," she managed.

Derek put their lunch on the counter that delineated the kitchen area, a galley set up in one corner of the beamed room. "It met my needs. Out here, I live simply."

"So it appears."

"I can see it's not what you expected."

"You seem pleased."

Damn, she was making him flush. "It's a change for me, that's all. I just brought what I could haul myself."

"A few pieces of furniture to go with the state-of-the-art sound system and the yacht in the driveway."

"Teak—"

"I apologize. I'm not usually sarcastic. It's just that if I'm twenty-eight, that makes you thirty, a little old to be living so simply."

"Expectations again."

"I didn't have any expectations. I have no idea what your tastes are except in cars. Judging by the hot little model you drive, I would have guessed this would be sophisticated, contemporary."

"You've misjudged me."

"No cutting edge?" She turned her frank stare on him.

"Disappointed?"

"I'd have liked to see some examples of your work."

"My portfolio's in Skerrystead."

"You seem relieved. I'm not interested in judging you. As a matter of fact, I hadn't given your life-style a thought."

"Cutting edge." He arched a brow. "Sorry to disappoint you. The shoemaker in this case goes barefoot." Derek busied himself with putting lunch on plates, an ancient chipped set from the Skerry-stead pantry. Teak's silences spoke volumes and made him analyze every word that left her tantalizing mouth. As he laid out pickles, she came next to him. "Tea or coffee?"

"Tea's fine."

"Would you put two mugs of water in the microwave?" Once again, he attempted to keep the conversation innocuous. "Make mine coffee. It's there on the shelf."

"Sugar?"

"Black, please."

They touched occasionally—an elbow, a shoulder, nearly a hip. Each brush sent a fresh surge through him. She seemed oblivious.

When the drinks were made, Teak slid aside a mound of sailing and design magazines from the coffee table to make room for their plates, then settled into the couch.

"Why give this up?"

"You do cut right to the bone."

"You invited me to lunch. We could talk about the weather if you'd rather."

He sipped his coffee. "No, of course not. It's time to move on."

"Home to Skerrystead is moving on? Sounds more like escape. Anything as dramatic as a broken love affair?"

Derek narrowed his glance as she chewed innocently, smiling at him over her sandwich.

"Are you fishing for a confession?"

She swallowed. "Just trying to fill in the gaps from these past few years."

"Let's just say the time is right for the move."

"Literally and figuratively?" They exchanged glances.

"Both."

"Your lease expired?"

"Yup."

"Have your creative juices dried up out here?"

"Are you going for the jugular?"

She laughed. "Not intentionally. You're hedging on your love life so I'm focusing on the creative process."

"A wise move." He began to relax as she wriggled a pink-socked foot up under her and settled back into the cushion. Derek tried to figure out how a wild-haired boatyard owner who'd arrived in a diesel truck could ooze femininity from every flannel and denim-covered pore.

"I'm sure it ebbs and flows," she was saying.

"My love life?"

"Did you want to talk about that? I thought we had to stick to furniture."

"We do. It does. There's enough traditional stuff—repairs, bookcases—to keep it more flow than ebb. Most of my design work is for clients off the Cape."

"So you've said. Long haul from out here at the tip, in to the mainland."

"Long haul. I just finished with my last local project, cabinets for a retired professor. I designed some bookcases and an entertainment center for his study."

"What makes you think Skerrystead will suit you better?"

"Why shouldn't it?"

She leaned into the cushions and finished a pickle. "It depends on your life-style, your needs. The off season has a hollowness that's tough to fill."

"I'm not afraid of solitude."

"Have you ever been there after Labor Day?"

"To be honest, no."

"Solitude describes it, that's for sure. It was tough growing up. First of all you and the rest of the summer folks pulled out. Your houses sat battened and boarded. Then school started. That was hard as a teenager because another chunk left for boarding school. The harbor emptied from a mass of pleasure boats to winter sticks marking the moorings till spring. Nobody's left except the commercial fishermen who're hungry enough to tough out the winter, and the cranberry growers."

"It's a little late to tell me there's not much to look forward to."

"Sea gulls, naked trees and deserted beaches. Not much for inspiration."

Derek walked to the hearth and put the screen in front of the logs. "You might be surprised at what inspires me. Solitude can be invigorating."

"But you're a craftsman. There's darn little to feed the soul." Teak looked startled by her own wistfulness. Another pause hung between them. She cleared her throat. "I would assume your soul needs a fair amount of nurturing to stay creative."

A small spot beneath his breastbone began to warm. He hadn't asked her to lunch to talk about his soul. "Inspiration comes from surprising sources."

She blinked. "How about that look at your workshop?"

He pointed at the raised panel door behind her. "The shop's through there. Help yourself."

He waited as she rose, all curves and angles, smelling faintly of dill and some perfume that reminded him oddly of summer. He followed. She perused the space. With the exception of clients, he rarely shared this, especially with women who knew his background. He watched Teak walk to the workbench and waited for the inevitable return to the topic of who he was, where he'd come from, what he'd given up for *this*.

Instead, she touched a set of chisels. Her fingers were slender, without rings, her nails filed into small semicircles. As she ran her hand over the well-worn handles, the intimacy of the gesture tightened his gut.

"Those were a gift," he offered. "From a retired cabinetmaker named Andrew Davies, a Welshman I apprenticed under in Connecticut."

"These had been his?"

"Brought with him from Wales in 1946 when he emigrated."

"Quite an honor." She fixed her brown eyes on him. "He must have recognized a kindred spirit."

Derek countered with a smile. "Still sizing me up?"

"In a manner of speaking, I suppose I am. I'll bet that you're an excellent craftsman."

There was that wash of adrenaline again. "It's what I do."

"I suspect it's what you love."

"It is what I love, although I've been accused of knowing nothing about the emotion."

"By those who know you?"

In an effort to change her focus, Derek put his hand on Teak's shoulder. Immediately a flush crept from the hollow of her throat, deeper than any he'd seen before. "What does it take to feed *your* soul, Teak?"

"You're changing the subject again."

"Damn right, I am."

She paused to inhale. "Somebody's broken your heart."

"I was asking about your soul. You're the youngest Brewster, twenty-eight, you said. Has it been all work? Hasn't there been anybody in that yard young enough to give you a run for your money?"

"The boatyard? Of course not."

"But you do make time for both?"

"I keep them separate."

Conflicting emotions tore at him. The urge to keep her at arm's length was being swallowed by the desire to kiss her. His mouth tingled and before his better judgment surfaced, he bent to her lips. Teak's mouth was closed, but warm, soft and pliant. The sound of his name in soft surprise was barely a whisper. Desire danced down her spine.

He parted her lips with his tongue. Her fingers were cool against his neck, then warm as she moved over his shirt, across his shoulder blades. Pleasure rippled through him, radiating from her touch. It was enough to stand there and let his body soak it up. He brushed her hair, her jaw, her neck, and fantasized of places far more erotic. He closed his eyes and envisioned her fingers tracing the chisel handles. Touching her brought him back in touch with himself. He'd been too long without this. He had to clear his throat before he could speak.

Five

———

"**P**lease don't do that again," Teak said softly.

"Would you consider staying for the rest of the afternoon?"

Slowly Teak shook her head.

"There's a fire to tend and a beach to walk. With this economy and the off-season, the restaurants are begging for customers."

She was still trying to catch her breath. "Tempting, but I don't think so. It's not a good idea."

"How could something that feels this good not be a fabulous idea?"

Derek's eyes seemed to absorb the light as he looked at her and she took half a step backward, turning toward the window. "You're moving to Skerrystead."

"Within arm's length."

"This is already too much mixing of business with pleasure."

"Storing my boat is the only business I have with you. Pleasure is another topic altogether."

She blew her bangs away from her face. "I'm not interested in anything more than business and the friendship that's developed. You have a hell of a way of kissing, Derek. I knew you would."

"Don't tell me you've been fantasizing."

"It's something I've been curious about since I can remember."

"Satisfying an old curiosity?"

"Yes." The moment she realized she had him at a loss for words, she smiled and stepped past him into the living room. Her heart was thundering so violently she was sure he could hear it. Although she was gasping softly, she added with as much firmness as she could muster, "You were asking about my private life. It's in fine shape. As I said, it's removed from the yard, and the yard is where I'm headed. There's a boat out there to be delivered to Skerrystead."

"I suppose if you and I are going to rattle around empty Skerrystead all winter, bumping into each other at the grocery store and the dentist's office, I should agree with you.''

Teak thought about correcting him, but questions about her own plans and expectations would put her on the defensive. With Derek Tate she wanted—needed—to be the one doing the questioning. Instead she asked for the bathroom.

''Through the bedroom,'' he said finally as he picked up the lunch plates from the coffee table.

The bathroom was clean but cluttered with shaving equipment on the counter. The bath mat was on the floor, and she could make out a damp footprint. A towel hung over the shower curtain. The intimacy made her shiver.

She ran cold water on her wrists and sat down on the edge of the bathtub, face in hands. Inside of her a fifteen-year-old was doing handsprings and calling, *He kissed me!* She stood up and splashed her cheeks. In the other room was no fresh-faced, teenage, rich man's son hell-bent on stealing kisses.

Out there in that shabby living room was a fascinating combination of power and reserve, humility, talent, defiance and drive, not to mention raw sexuality. Teak groaned and splashed her face again as much to cool off her curiosity as her desire.

Derek Tate's love life, career and obvious restlessness were none of her business. She'd kissed him. She'd liked it. She'd satisfied her curiosity. Enough!

She left the bathroom decidedly cooler and clearer of head. Resolve was everything. Between the bathroom and the main room, a queen-size, four-poster bed sat against the windowed bedroom wall. Pillows had been plumped and tossed at the head, over the fluff of a down comforter, slightly askew.

Teak stood at the foot. The frame was cherry, rubbed to a glowing patina, ending in tapered legs. The base of the posts were carved in scallop shells. The headboard tapered into a design that mimicked the shape. Had she seen the bed in the Tates' Skerrystead house she would have assumed it was an antique or a family heirloom. She skimmed her hand over the blanket rail and knelt.

"Beautiful," she whispered to herself. As she spoke, she ran her fingers over the shell on the post and slid her hand under the comforter. Two raised shells merged in the middle of the footboards. Carved into the left was DRT. The right shell was marred by a single gouge, left raw and unfinished, the obvious beginning of a second set of initials.

Curiosity ate at her as she replaced the comforter. Through the door she could hear Derek clattering the dishes at the sink. How little she knew of the man. How much she had conjured from her own imagination.

At five o'clock Thursday afternoon Derek massaged his lower back and looked from his window across the water to the island mass that was Martha's Vineyard. Like its neighbors on Breaker's Point, the Tate family cottage was an oversize, understated throwback to the pre-Depression era in which it had been built. The Tates' waterfront neighborhood hugged the undulating shoreline of Vineyard Sound, literally turning its back on the village—and on the year-round residents whose only access to the coastline was town beaches and municipal waterfront.

He turned from the window and looked at his bed, dismantled and reassembled with the rest of his meager belongings in the Skerrystead bedroom. There had been a time when he'd felt as though the single gouge in the unfinished shell had been carved in his chest. He glanced at the footboard, tossed the comforter onto the bare mattress and left the house.

Ethan Brewster, Proprietor swayed on its hinges as Derek eased his car into the nearly deserted lot of the boatyard. The nip in the air had turned serious, and he hunkered into his sweater as a gust swirled in from between the sheds.

He followed the breeze to number two. His sloop was propped on its permanent jacks, balanced by wooden blocks that had *TATE* spelled out in sloppy strokes from someone's paintbrush years earlier. As long as a Brewster had owned the yard, there'd been at least one Tate craft of some sort wintered here, more often than not two or three. Teak was standing at the bow, shivering in a chamois shirt as she looked up at the neglected handrail. He drank in the sight of her.

"Teak Brewster, a master with steel wool and varnish," she was muttering.

He stepped forward, inches from her ear. "Looking for something to feed your soul?"

She pivoted directly into his chest. "You scared the life out of me!"

He held her at arm's length and laughed. "I can see that. I thought you heard me come in."

She took a step backward. "I wasn't expecting you—anybody, for that matter. What are you doing here?"

"Here in town?"

"For starters."

"Getting my house in order. Moving beds and boxes."

"What are you doing out here?"

"Checking up on the boatyard owner, seeing if she got my sloop onto the jacks in one piece."

"Why is it that every man who walks in here is skeptical?" She gestured with a swing of her arm. "I moved your boat. Without a scratch."

"Impressive. You are one impressive woman, Teresa Brewster."

"I'm doing what needs to be done."

"That's all this boatyard means to you?"

"It's lock-up time, Derek. I'm tired and on my way home."

"No answer to my soul-feeding question?"

She shivered but declined the offer of his arm as they walked toward her truck. "This season my soul will be fed by the knowledge that I'm keeping the Brewsters ahead of the creditors."

"You're a close-knit family. You're dad was a widower, as I recall. When did you lose your mother?"

"When I was ten. Part of the reason Pop had us working out here was to keep an eye on us."

"Dana, Molly and Teak Brewster. Where was I all those Skerrystead summers that I didn't know one of you from the other?"

It was a rhetorical question to which they both knew the answer. Teak opened the door to her truck. "You might say we were on the same road, just different lanes. You were always in the passing lane, Derek. I spent most of those years on the shoulder."

He laughed.

She climbed into the seat and turned the key in the ignition." In fact, it might be that we were headed in opposite directions."

Derek closed Teak's door as she turned over the engine. "Dinner?"

"Excuse me?"

"We both have to eat. You turned me down once this week. I've got a refrigerator full of groceries and a decent kitchen."

"I don't think—"

"Nothing else. Just food and decent conversation."

She arched her eyebrows and smiled. "Really?"

"I could use some decent conversation."

"Food and conversation. I'll swear to it if you will."

"You drive a hard bargain. Come out to the Point and eat with me. I'm not half bad in the culinary department, unless I can find someone willing to cook for me."

Her laugh animated her face. "It's not enough that I hauled your boat from one end of the Cape to the other?"

"For Teak Brewster, that was business as usual."

"You never wanted to kiss me in the first place. You're desperate for a cook."

"I admit I'm damned tired of my own cooking."

"What's in your refrigerator?"

"That would take what's left of the fun out of it."

She drummed her fingers on the steering wheel before finally turning to him. "No passes, and I'll *help* make dinner."

"What the heck. A person has to eat."

Derek savored sweet anticipation all the way out to Breaker's Point. Anticipation, however, was tempered by an uncharacteristic wave of self-consciousness as he approached his house. Teak Brewster probably had an opinion about the neighborhood, one, no doubt, she'd be only too happy to share. Half a dozen times he checked his rearview mirror and watched her follow in the pickup truck. The woman had a way of weaving implication and vague referrals into every conversation. Desire had a way of weaving itself into every confrontation.

He parked under the portico in the front and she pulled in next to him. With the Indian summer sun teasing the treetops, Derek led her toward the side of the house.

"Ah, the service entrance," she murmured. "There used to be a discreet little sign with an arrow pointing to this door."

His ears burned as he slipped the key in the lock. "Groceries were delivered in those days." He blanched. "You didn't work here, did you?"

"As a matter of fact—"

"Oh, God."

"Things haven't changed a bit." She crossed the room and grinned at him. "I take that back. You got rid of the stove with the broken burner, and somebody's put in a microwave oven." She pointed to a wall of doors. "If I remember correctly, pantry, back stairs and that door leads to a maid's room and bath."

"Why didn't you say something?"

"Say something?"

"Help," he muttered as he swore under his breath.

"*Help,* as in, was I one of the help, or help me out of this awkward situation?"

"It's one and the same, isn't it? Hell, I ask you to dinner and you know your way around this kitchen as well as I do."

She faltered. "Look, Derek, you know who I am and where I come from. I know who you are and a lot of where you've been. If you're going to stumble all over yourself because you're afraid you've asked the maid to dinner, you'd better walk me out to my truck."

"Teak, I was only thinking of you."

"Maybe I'm too self-conscious here."

"Don't be."

"I didn't mean to be snide."

"You should have given me some warning." Impulsively he put his hands on her shoulders. "Or was that the point? To come out here and make things awkward?"

Six

Teak shivered under his touch. "No. I never..."
She leaned and touched his cheek.

The next thing she knew, his mouth was pressing
hers and his arms were around her. Her shock
melted into desire as dangerous as frayed wire.
Derek's tongue trailed across the delicate lining of
her mouth. She felt his hands press the small of her
back. Her breasts molded to the contours of his
chest. He rocked gently and her body sweetened the
pressure. She dragged in a breath as heat tore
through her.

She kissed him briefly, instinctively, fully aware

of how wonderful it felt, unaware until she gasped and pulled away how tightly she had been clinging to him. "We had a deal," she cried.

"One you don't like any more than I do."

"You're wrong."

He backed away, across the kitchen. "Then I'll stick to it, if it kills me." His blue eyes were dark, his mouth tight. "But first I want to know why you agreed to come out here."

She tried to make her gaze as devoid of desire as possible. "That same old curiosity. You've been a charmer all your life, Derek. You still are."

He didn't look flattered. "I would have remembered you, dammit. If I'd ever seen you working in this house, I would have remembered you. I, at least, would have known your were Bud's daughter."

She caught her breath. "Is that meant as a compliment?"

"It's meant as fact. You've fascinated me since I walked into the boatyard three weeks ago. There's something incredibly sexy about a woman who can sling insults and smooth grizzled egos at the same time."

"Yours?"

"I meant Manny's, but I suppose I fit into the same category. There's something damned intriguing about a woman who sidesteps compliments and hides behind wit and sharp words."

Teak's heart leaped, and she ran her hand through her hair. She forced her gaze to stay steady. His was unreadable. It doubled her pulse. Derek turned to the refrigerator and pulled out green peppers, chicken breasts and a bottle of sauce. All the while she was quiet. The silence crackled.

He yanked out a head of broccoli. "I wish you'd say something clever and sarcastic to clear the air."

"About that kiss, or your fear that I was hired help around here?"

"Start wherever you like."

"I'll start where we should have the day you found me so *fascinating*. There's always been two sides to Skerrystead—those who have it all, and those who work for those who have it all."

"Hell, Teak—"

"You asked, Derek. There's no sense in pretending you and I are anything but what we are. You're the water view, I'm the sand hills. Stop blushing, and hand me the broccoli." She took it from him and put it on the counter. "We're all grown up. At the moment I run the boatyard that stores your family's yachts. I'm a woman. Both of those things set me apart. If I were a female executive at Tate Electronics, you wouldn't give me a second glance."

"You're dead wrong on that score. Forget Tate. This situation's bad enough and all you're doing is storing my boat. You are who you are, my father's firm or your father's boatyard. The whole package is fascinating.''

"Derek, really.''

"You've been doing your damnedest to stay one step ahead of me since the day we met. I'm just intrigued and egotistical enough to sit back most of the time and listen, but I'm as good a judge of character as you are. You're a hell of a woman, Teak, but you're also too self-conscious about the differences between our backgrounds.''

"Can you blame me?''

"No. But I can work up a darn good fury if you've set me up tonight in order to protect yourself. Since that first day at the boatyard I've been embarrassed that I don't remember you. It gives you an edge. I wish to hell you'd stop getting so much enjoyment out of it.''

"It isn't enjoyment, it's self-defense.''

Chagrin deepened his complexion. "I guess I deserve this.''

"Deserve what?''

"This. The perfect setup. The fact that you came out here tonight to embarrass me.''

"Think what you like. You know good and well you brought me here to see how fast you could get me upstairs. Deal or no deal.''

"That wasn't my intention, but if you're willing, I'm not going to pretend I don't want you.''

She exhaled slowly. "Is it always that easy for you?"

"There's nothing easy about this situation!"

"There was a time when I would have done anything you'd asked to hold your attention. Those days are gone. I'm no starry-eyed teenager offering sex to keep you interested. Not that you ever had a clue, thank heavens."

"I was a fool."

"You were a kid. So was I."

"And now we're adults. Any suggestions as to where we go from here?"

"Derek, I never intended to come here for anything but dinner."

"Then forgive me for giving in to my primitive instincts and I'll forgive you for enjoying it."

"This is where I should sputter and protest that I didn't."

He smiled. "You're not one for lying."

"Dinner, Tate."

"Right. Help me make some. It'll keep my hands busy."

She laughed. "Forgive my stream of consciousness. I'd forgotten that there are as many memories for me here as there are for you at the boatyard."

"I need to know what kind."

"Why?"

"Because I'm not out to hurt you."

Teak made a pretense of searching for a frying pan. She squatted in front of a cabinet until Derek's touch brought her up on her feet. She held a pot lid between them. "My memories have nothing to do with reality. I outgrew Skerrystead and my illusions a long time ago. You're a reminder of them."

"But you're still in town."

"Out of love and necessity."

"For Bud?"

"Yes. For the man my father was, a guy who worked every day of his life to give us what you take for granted. I was an angry, mean kid a lot of the time, and he never gave up on me, never stopped working toward his dream for us."

"You don't know how lucky you are."

"Yes, I do. When I see a millionaire's son tinkering at carpentry, playing at being working class—"

"Just a minute!"

"—furnishing his cottage with cheap castoffs and chipped china, yet jumping from place to place when the mood hits, all the while hauling a twenty-three-foot yacht behind him, I get defensive. When that same person kisses me senseless—whether I enjoy it or not—I get *very* defensive."

"I kissed you because you're so damned appealing."

"Don't go off on a tangent. I'm talking about yachts and chipped china."

"Continue."

"Thank you. This is the nineties," she said evenly. "I'm not about to jump under the covers, despite the fact that you're still as gorgeous, sexy and appealing as you ever were." He fought a smile. "Am I?"

"You're living up to your reputation."

"*Reputation.* That's all you know of me." He crossed the floor to the breakfast area and looked out toward the pool. When he finally turned around, he leaned against the sill. "God knows there are years I'm not particularly proud of. My adolescence was an open book. When you're fourteen and your parents' divorce settlement makes *Time* magazine, you don't have much of a private life. Seventeen and your old man's on the cover of *Paris Match* and *International Business Week,* you lose your perspective. He was at Camp David advising the president during my last father-son weekend at prep school. He was in Geneva on an economic mission when I graduated, but then, you don't build a financial empire by spending time with your children. You throw money at them to keep them from complaining."

"You had plenty to spend."

"Remember the summer he bailed out Jason and the Atoms? The hottest rock group in America gets burned out of their hotel in Hyannis and my old man has the clout to put them up in this house for two days so they could keep their performance schedule. He paid the entire Skerrystead police force's overtime so the group'd have guaranteed security, not to mention caterers to feed them and a driver and limousine to get them to the stage and back.''

"I remember." She waited as he crossed the room to her.

"After that I had girls crawling in my bedroom window, sleeping in my car." Derek winced, then surprised her by leaning against the pantry door and sliding to the floor. He looked heavenward. "Please tell me you weren't one."

He felt Teak slide down next to him.

"I wasn't."

"Thank God." He brought his knees up and propped his forehead against the worn denim for a moment. Desire teased again.

"For me you were pure fantasy," she said softly. "You're right that I knew only your reputation. Reality was only being scraped up off Harbor Street or watching you in the boatyard hanging around your yachts or signing your father's name on charges for racing equipment."

"Somewhere along the line my brother discovered that he rarely read the bills, just paid them."

"You spent a lot of time at the yard."

"There were damn few places I loved as a kid. The yard was one. One of these days Manny'll remember that he caught me shoplifting in your front room. It was the year my mother moved my brothers and me to Seattle and sent us east for the summer without her. She never came back to Skerrystead."

"I know."

"You and the world. After that there wasn't a whole lot of discipline on good old Cape Cod. Summers consisted of housekeepers, glimpses of Dad, and me and my brother getting away with murder."

"What did you steal?"

"A life jacket."

"That's one way to express your anger."

Derek laughed. "Can you believe it? There wasn't a thing in the store my old man wouldn't have paid for. I suppose I was trying to prove something to myself, but I wasn't even smart enough to shove something small into my pocket so I'd get away with it."

"Maybe you weren't trying to get way with it. Maybe you wanted your parents to sit up and take notice. If big bad Pop had kicked you off the premises for stealing and had you hauled into the police station, your parents would have had to bail you out, to discuss their incorrigible son. They'd have had to get together."

"You have the perfect reasoning power of a screwed-up fourteen-year-old." Derek looked at Teak as he leaned his head against the wall. He closed his eyes and tried to figure out what had compelled him to spill his guts.

Teak's shoulder brushed his as she murmured, "It's just as well that you never knew me. We would have made a very dangerous couple back then."

Derek touched her face and fought his need to kiss her. "You're incredibly right about me, but very wrong about yourself. You wouldn't have given in to me, not for a minute. Back then the whole world was saying yes. You would have been the *no.*"

"You would have left me in the sand for somebody else."

"I would have loved you for it."

Something softened in her eyes. She shook her head slowly which pressed her temple into his open hand. Her hair brushed his palm. He ran his knuckles against her cheek.

"I can't touch you, Derek," she whispered.

"Touching's the easy part," he whispered.

"Easier than building a relationship? Easier than friendship?"

Her words slapped him again. He leaned to her and brushed her mouth. He thought about the door behind her, about the back staircase and the

countless times he'd snuck up and down on clan-
destine summer nights. The top step still squeaked.
He thought of the bed hauled from Wellfleet, set up
in the room off the wide landing, with the water
view across Nantucket Sound. His room, his bed,
the thick down comforter as soft as her breasts...
Making love to her would be infinitely easier than
this.

She shifted to her knees and stood up. "Coming
here was a mistake. I need to leave before we're
completely out of control. I had no intention..."
She shook her head and looked at him. "We've said
enough about intentions. No chicken, no peppers,
no fire when the sun goes down. It's time that I
went home where I belong."

Derek stood up. "I need that answer."

"About my relationship to this house?" She
started for the door. "The summer I was sixteen I
dated a dockhand from the harbor named Steve
Morani. Your cousin Brad asked us here to a party.
A bunch of us wound up making pizza here in the
kitchen. That's how I know this room."

"You were here as a guest?" His complexion
darkened. "You weren't working here at the time?"

"No. I never had a job except at the boatyard."

"What the hell was all that innuendo? You let me
stumble all over myself thinking you were one of
our maids."

"Derek, you're a genius at jumping to your own conclusions."

"Conclusions you laid at my feet. It was a logical assumption."

"About as logical as thinking Pop would kick you out of the boatyard and have you thrown in jail." She opened the back door and gestured for him to stay where he was.

"If you spent the better part of a night in this house, where the hell was I?"

"Don't lose sleep over it while you eat your chicken. It was just another night. Derek, we are what we are and who we are. In Skerrystead there's no getting around it. There's too much of my past tied up in you for me ever to be comfortable. It's not that I *won't,* it's that I *can't* be just another notch in your bed." She threw the euphemism at him she as she left and was halfway down Breaker's Point before she remembered the gouge in the shell.

Seven

Teak looked at the bills laid out on the desk in front of her, tempted to toss them in the air and pay the first one that drifted to the floor.

She entered them in the bookkeeping file. Profit was the bottom line. Keeping Brewster Boatyard in the black was the only way she would get a decent offer for it.

She massaged her neck muscles as she worked, unaware of the wistful smile as her hand slid under her collar. Worrying wasn't going to pay the rent. Neither was continual daydreaming about stolen moments in the kitchen on Breaker's Point. Giving up everything she'd worked for in New York to keep the boatyard running had been painful enough. Continual, unappreciated thoughts of Derek Tate did nothing to improve her disposition. Maybe she should just jump into bed with him, satisfy her curiosity and get on with her life. She moved her hand abruptly.

It had been two days since she'd left the man wondering where he'd been that night so long ago when she'd socialized in his kitchen. Derek Tate then, Derek Tate now... It was enough to drive a woman to distraction.

Sandwich in hand, she left for the storeroom to unpack a shipment of flotation cushions. She should be at one of her Manhattan power lunches discussing business, or perusing a Greenwich Village gallery with a colleague. If her fellow financial wizards could see her now...

Her reverie was interrupted by the sound of her name on the yard's paging system, and she dusted herself off as she returned to her office. A casually dressed man and woman in their late thirties were standing at her desk.

Teak offered her hand and introduced herself.

"I'm Paul Bendette, and this is my wife, Bay. We're hoping your yard handles wooden boat repair. We've come down from Alden's Cove to look at a twenty-two-foot Haglof out on Breaker's Point. She's a classic, but in need of some serious work on the stern post and some of the planks. We think the price is right, considering the condition, but we need a second opinion. The owner suggested that we check in with your yard.''

Halfway through the request Teak's heart sank. ''If it's engine work you need, or fiberglass—''

''That would be Manny Souza, our mechanic.''

Teak spun around at the sound of the familiar voice finishing her sentence. Derek Tate was offering his hand and ignoring her surprise. ''Otherwise, I'm the guy you want.'' He introduced himself. ''I specialize in cabinetry and furniture-making, but wooden boat repair is my first love.''

''Wonderful,'' Bay replied.

''You've had experience?'' Paul asked.

''I've been working out of Wellfleet, most recently. I did some repair work in Connecticut, but I've just relocated to Skerrystead. I can give you a full list of references, and I'd be happy to take a look at the boat and give you a professional opinion. In fact, if it's *Kestral*, the Hamilton boat out on the Point, it belongs to one of my neighbors. I've sailed it myself.''

''Could you give us an estimate?'' Bay asked.

''We'd be happy to,'' Derek replied.

We. Teak shot him another look. Derek ignored it.

As Teak listened, the Bendettes declared it to be a great idea and fortuitous coincidence. The four of them walked out to the parking lot.

Paul turned to Teak. "If we wind up buying the boat, I assume your yard can haul it here for the work and storage, and we can arrange for delivery to Alden's Cove in the spring?"

"Certainly. We're a full-service yard. We've stored *Kestral* in the past, as a matter of fact." Teak quoted storage fees as they walked. Next to her, Derek and Bay fell into social small talk. Teak kept half an ear on the conversation, which seemed to be comparisons of mutual friends in Newport.

"About eight years ago," Bay was saying. "Paul and I met at a party at Sea Mist the night before my brother Jeremy sailed in the Bermuda race."

"Son of a gun! I was at that party and I crewed that year on *Medallion*..."

Teak fought a twinge of jealousy at the social networking. Boats, engines, financial management she knew, but there was nothing she could add to chatter about Newport mansions and black-tie yachting parties.

Bay asked Derek if he had the time to follow them out to the Hamiltons'.

He nodded. "Absolutely."

The Bendettes got into their sports car. Teak waved them off and crossed the pavement to Derek who had already started his. "Before you buzz out to Breaker's Point and completely take over my job, how about an explanation?''

He grinned. ''I came over today to check on my own boat and see if I could talk you into a cup of coffee. I overheard the Bendettes. Simple as that, and a lucky break, huh? I'm not taking over your job. Your yard doesn't handle wooden boat repair.''

''I'm well aware of that,'' she muttered.

''Simple MBA basics. If you're going to pull this yard out of the doldrums, you've got to strike while the iron's hot. The Bendettes need the work done. You need the income. I need the commission.''

''From me? I'm to put you on commission when you bring me repairs we're not equipped to handle?''

''I'm equipped. Wooden boats *are* my first priority. They just don't come up enough to keep me from starving.''

''You've never mentioned wooden boats.''

''I've been too busy spilling my guts about my childhood.'' He rubbed his hand over his steering wheel. ''I still haven't figured out how you got all that out of me. I don't have much need to talk about that stuff.''

''Maybe the need is for someone to listen.''

He arched his brows and looked at his knuckles.

''Derek, simple MBA principles tell me to ask for proof that you're qualified to do what you're so blithely telling the Bendettes is your specialty. Not only that, but you told the Bendettes you'll work here. There's nothing in that shed but cobwebs."

"Shed three's perfect. Next to the machine shop."

"*My* reputation's at stake. Things are tough enough at the boatyard without taking on someone who's not qualified to do what he says he can. Besides, you've rented—"

"Teak, darling, *Kestral*'s twenty-two feet long. Even you would have a heck of a time backing her into the upholsterer's shop."

Teak, darling. Where the hell had that come from? Derek pondered his spontaneity for most of the drive out to the Hamilton place, less than a quarter of a mile from his own address. Teak Brewster *was* darling, of course, especially when she was baffled, disgruntled and racing to keep one step ahead of him. Rare moments. She was also elusive and smug.

Another notch in his bed. Long after she'd left his kitchen he'd tried to figure out if she'd pulled that caustic comment out of the air or if she knew about Hilary Gates and the hand-crafted marriage bed.

Reluctantly he pushed thoughts of the brunette aside as he pulled in behind the Bendettes. Business waited. Jane Hamilton, *Kestral*'s owner not only greeted him warmly, but vouched for his knowledge and skill and asked about his family. Paul and Bay seemed encouraged by the personal connection.

With the couple beside him, he looked the damage over thoroughly and assessed *Kestral*'s condition. Work, yes, but nothing he couldn't handle. He wrote his estimate on his business card after scratching out his former Wellfleet address and phone number. "Nothing's accurate but my name. I'm in transition at the moment."

"Relocating?"

"Just this week. I'll be living right around the bend." He nodded in the direction of the water.

"What a stroke of luck. We'd never have found you out on the other end of the Cape."

After another fifteen minutes of chat, Derek shook hands. In the interest of professionalism, he left the final purchase decisions between the Bendettes and the boat owner. The couple agreed to be in touch with him within the next few days.

Bay glanced at his card. "Should we reach you through the boatyard?"

"Either way. Teak and I are a team."

Twenty minutes later he found Teak in shed three, hands on her hips, shaking her head. She turned as he entered.

"The best I can do is sawhorses and a running account at the desk for your supplies."

"I've got my own setup-workbench, tools, lathes, everything."

She turned those luminescent eyes on him. "Derek, what if I don't want you working here?"

"Preposterous." He watched her hesitate and swallow whatever she was about to say. "Teak, use your business sense. Whatever else we are or aren't to each other, you need me professionally. You need the rent. I'll bring in clients."

"Can you afford a shop in both locations? How'll you make time to hold down two jobs?"

"Consolidation. One location. This is all I need."

"*This?* You plan to work here full-time?"

"It's the perfect solution for both of us."

"There's nothing perfect about it. I don't want you here underfoot."

"Too much mixing of business and pleasure? Forget about your hormones."

"My hormones! All they're doing is responding to yours." She mumbled an oath. "Forget I said that. Just leave my hormones out of it."

"Exactly. Look at the opportunity. Word of mouth is everything in this business. Bay and I made mutual connections. It turns out she's Bay *Chandler* Bendette."

"As in Chandler Sails?"

"None other. It's just that kind of connection this yard needs. A Chandler has repair work done in the Brewster boatyard, pretty soon they're recommending me—us—to their clients." His voice softened. *Us*.

Teak drummed her fingers on her thigh. "How long will it take to repair *Kestral?*"

"Not long if I put it ahead of my other projects."

"Then I'll use that as a trial. Four weeks. We start out on a trial basis."

"Four weeks! It's hardly worth setting up the lathes."

"From now until Thanksgiving. I also want strong references."

"Why the sudden scrutiny when it's obvious how much you stand to gain from this?"

"With the exception of your active social reputation, and your turbulent adolescence, what do I know about you?"

"I kiss well." He waited for a flush or sputter.

"I put that in the category of active social reputation," she replied without missing a beat. Her eyes danced, however. "I never hire a man based on his kissing ability."

"Wonderful. I was hoping Manny, Greg and John weren't my competition."

She drummed again against her jeans. He was delighted to see her fight a smile. "I want to see a portfolio of your work, if such a thing really exists. Derek, you admit you've jumped from place to place. Commitment is not a word I'd use to describe you. You've been in New York, you've been in Connecticut, then there was Wellfleet, now Skerrystead. How long have you ever lived in one place? Electronics, furniture, boats... This boatyard doesn't run on a whim the way your life does."

"It hasn't been the way it appears."

"Let's assume you *do* set up shop and build a client base. What happens when the old wanderlust returns, or boredom sets in again?"

"Give me some credit."

"For what? You don't know Skerrystead the way I do. It doesn't suit you, believe me."

"You're projecting, Teak. The one it doesn't suit is you."

Through the open door gulls called and a flock of geese honked as they circled the inlet edging the yard. "You're about as settled as those geese." She paused and looked at the empty space before looking directly into his eyes. "What happens when you're tired of trying to get me into bed?"

"We're keeping that separate, remember?"

"Who's to say you won't up and leave in February when it's too cold, too lonely, or I've turned you down one too many times? Suppose Newport begins to appeal to you, or Hyannis or Plymouth? *Pouf,* you're gone, and *our* clients are gone with you."

The humor had gone from her expression and Derek winced. "Is this really how you see me?"

"You've made wanderlust part of your lifestyle."

"I admit it's taken time to come up with something that gives me a sense of satisfaction. I've come to it late, but I've found it. It's not a whim. I've put everything I've got into my work. It's the same spirit that your dad had for this place."

"Leave Pop out of this."

"I'm asking you to trust me. What I feel for this place is the spirit I can see in you, Teak. I don't know why you said you'd outgrown Skerrystead the other night. You've put all your energy into this place, too. I'm just sorry I didn't know that a few years back. But who knows? We might make a great work team as well as lovers."

"Derek, you don't seem to understand."

"Understand?"

"I haven't been working here for years. I just started last month. I came back when Pop died to keep the yard from going under. Brewster Boatyard is on the market. It's for sale. I'm only here till the first of the year, trying to pump life into it to make a decent profit."

Derek took a short, shallow breath as if the wind had been knocked out of him. "You're selling this?"

"It's been on the market since last spring. How on earth could you think that this is my career? I'm doing what needs to be done, that's all."

"I had no idea."

Teak's voice rose and echoed in the empty shed. Wind rattled the corrugated metal. "If you set up shop in here, you're part of the sale. I don't want anything in the yard that won't remain available to the buyer."

"I'm part of the package?"

"That's up to you. You can do what you want with joinery, but if you establish a quality repair shop for wooden boats, yes. The real estate climate is soft enough without my having to qualify what stays and what doesn't."

"What happens in January if it hasn't sold?"

"We find a manager to take over until it does or I get another leave from my office."

"I had no idea."

"It's really none of your concern."

"But you are."

"As a temporary diversion, maybe. Knock off the flattery, please. Don't stretch your already fragile credibility by handing me more lines. I don't know what fantasies you've been weaving, but you and I both know in the end you're still Breaker's Point. I'm still the sand hills. No amount of heavy breathing in that bed of yours will change that."

"I don't care about changing it."

"Good, because come January, somebody else will be giving you orders from that office over there. The chances that it'll be another woman are pretty slim."

"Is this what you want? Do you know what you're doing? I can't believe this boatyard is on the block."

"I'm doing what has to be done. Money's the only reason I'm back in this shuttered-for-the-season enclave of tight-lipped swamp Yankees."

Eight

Derek leaned on the sawhorse and swore.

"Don't look so shocked. You know me only from these yards, from Skerrystead. I have another life, Derek. I've been away from this for a long time."

"I don't believe it."

"Maybe you ought to come to grips with the fact that you're chasing after someone you don't even know. I gave up my fantasies long ago, but you're making me up as you go along."

"What could be more satisfying than hydraulic yacht hauling and computerized inventories?"

"Any number of things."

"What's more inspiring than the dunes and the gulls and the Cape off-season?"

"Just about anything in New York, in any season."

"City?"

"Manhattan. The Big Apple."

"You're a longshoreman working the piers?"

"I'm a CPA for Seavers and Cohn." She laughed as he digested the information.

"My god, they're Tate Electronics' auditors."

"I know."

"Bud Brewster's daughter's on Wall Street?"

"Eight years. I've been living on West Eighty-second Street, although I've sublet it for the time being."

His surprise was so genuine it transposed his features. For the first time since she'd known Derek Tate, he looked vulnerable. The moment passed as he cleared his throat. "Skerrystead to New York and back. I suppose you feel you've made a hell of a sacrifice."

"Yes, but for once the timing was right. My department is restructuring. I'm on a leave of absence, although I'm in touch by phone, and I'll be going back regularly for consultations."

"That's a mighty full schedule."

She shrugged. "You do what you have to do for the people you love. I have nieces and nephews facing college. I need a nest egg for my own children."

"You left some back on the Upper West Side?"

"You know what I mean."

"I thought until this conversation I had some idea. Now, frankly, I'm clueless."

"I want a family, the same as anyone else." She raised her hand and smiled in spite of the tension. "When I'm good and ready."

"And you've found some uptight, pin-striped power broker with good genes who has clawed his way up the social and financial ladders rung by rung, just as you have?"

His words stung. She stared into his troubled expression and tried to shake off the appraisal. "Skip the analysis."

"Or are you're avoiding Skerrystead because you're searching Manhattan's elite for someone who won't know that you grew up in a boatyard?"

"I explained it the other night."

"You explained your father's sacrifice and determination. At every turn you tell me I'm waterfront, you're sand hills. Teak, I understand more about you than you realize. What's got me baffled is that through all this soul-searching—not the least of which has been *mine,* thanks to you—you've never said a word about some ulcer-inducing, fast-track career in New York, let alone a master plan for husband, children and their college tuition."

"Hasn't it occurred to you that you're so busy kissing me that you haven't bothered with simple conversation?"

"Simple's not a word I would use to describe anything about you, Teak."

"It's very simple. I'm doing what has to be done."

"Even at the expense of your own happiness?"

"Maybe that depends on how you define the word. Right now I'll settle for a sense of satisfaction. I'm very satisfied at the choices I've made. You'd better take a closer look at yours. Take some time to think over your magnanimous offer to set up shop in here. At the risk of sounding incredibly egotistical, if you were doing it to continue your campaign to get me between the sheets, you've made a huge mistake. I won't be here after the New Year."

Between them a beam of rectangular light angled from window to cement floor. Derek pushed the sawhorse into it and slung his thigh up to balance himself. "Sorry to deflate your ego, but believe me, you or any woman between my sheets has nothing to do with my work. It's something we'd both enjoy, but it's separate from what I'm proposing. I made that mistake once. Never again."

"I'm relieved." She wasn't relieved. She was confused by her turmoil and the ache that refused to subside. Despite her words, it was the pull of the yard, the quiet beauty of the New England town that had kept her off balance since her first week back.

Derek Tate had no right to stroll into her life and deepen that ache. He was far safer as a fantasy than this flesh-and-blood combination of creativity and determination. She couldn't imagine the man within sighing distance every working day, even for two months. It wasn't client loyalty or guarantees to a future buyer she was worried about. It was her affection for Skerrystead and the man himself. Derek Tate made her flesh too warm and her pulse too jumpy.

To make the boatyard a smooth-running operation, she'd sacrificed too much without dropping a wrench into the works. "You'll do better at the upholsterer's shop," she tried.

"That's not what I want, now that I've got the chance to pull in boat accounts."

"Derek, it's what I want."

"Because I got too close just now? You can sit in my kitchen all smug, dropping hints and allusions to make me damned uncomfortable, but the minute *I* start using ten-cent psychology, you want me on the other end of town."

"I always did."

The sunlight played over his shoulder and pooled at his feet as he lowered his voice. "You want me the same place I want you, if only for the moment."

"No, I don't. That was teenage fantasy. I never was—and never will be—a just-for-the-moment person."

"Put that aside then, if you can. Tell me you're willing to give up this boat account and its potential because of hormones. That hardly seems like the woman you want me to think you are."

"You're baiting me."

"I want this space, with or without you."

Teak tried to keep her voice level and was disgusted that she had to clear her throat against the lump in it. "You understand it's our customers I worry about."

"I understand a lot more than you think."

Damn.

He brushed her sleeve. "I'm sorry for the cheap analysis, but you deserve a taste of your own medicine."

"There's no point in my pretending to be anything I'm not, especially with you."

"What would it take to persuade you to consider my apology and our work contract over a decent meal? We never had that dinner."

"In a public spot?"

"I was thinking more along the lines of my kitchen."

"I bet you were."

He was grinning at her. "I intend to keep trying."

"I'll eat with you."

"I'll be damned."

"At the Winsor Inn."

"You want me in a jacket and tie?"

"I'll dress up if you will."

"You don't trust my cooking."

Teak smiled. It was impossible not to. "Your cooking is the least of my worries."

They did eat. She insisted on meeting him at the restaurant and he spent a good portion of the first twenty minutes trying not to stare at her. The Winsor Inn was nearly deserted. They were seated at a corner table in the smallest of the dining rooms. A fire crackled on the hearth. Across the table Teak seemed to absorb the heat and the glow of the flames as she talked. Above the white linen tablecloth, her hair shimmered, her face shone. She had on makeup and a lamb's wool dress that clung and swung in ways he wanted to memorize.

After weeks of seeing her in jeans and sweaters, the effect was magnetic. Derek studied her pale peach shoulders in an effort to keep from getting lost in the depths of her deep brown eyes.

"New York," he said over his salad. "I never would have pegged you for city life."

"I'm not one for being pegged."

A log shifted, sending a spray of embers against the fire screen. Derek swirled his wine. "Who is Teresa Brewster?"

She sipped and watched him over the rim of her glass. "A hardworking CPA temporarily running a boatyard. A woman taking one day at a time."

"I agreed with the last part a few weeks back."

"And now?"

"Forget right now. Tell me about New York. Tell me how you got there. Tell me *why* you got there."

"There's no mystery. I went to college. I studied finance. I finished my graduate work through my employer. Seavers and Cohn has a wonderful program of benefits, including continuing education. I'm a CPA for them."

"In love with what you do?"

"Few people feel that strongly about their professions."

"That's not what I asked."

"I make an excellent salary."

"Is there a pin-striped power broker in your life?"

"No."

"Do you make the time for one?"

"I have a full, exciting and very challenging life."

"Euphemisms for stressed to the limits?"

"Of course there's stress. It goes with the territory. There's stress running the boatyard, for that matter."

"A different kind."

"True. In this situation I'm the one responsible for keeping the whole blasted business afloat."

"Is it that bad?" Derek waited as she considered the question. He took another sip and the liquid warmed him as he swallowed. He was in no hurry. Dinner could take all night if it maintained this mood of comfortable intimacy.

The physical pull he'd felt the first morning he'd seen her had never left him. Although it was nothing he gave a name to, nothing he sat and analyzed, being in the same room with her satisfied something bone-deep. He watched her and realized it wasn't sexual. Despite the flip remarks about his bed, it was something deeper. The need was bittersweet, like the pleasure he took from his work.

Teak leaned forward slightly, so that the light caressed the planes of her face. "Dwelling on whether it's bad or whether it's what I want to be doing, or even if I can ultimately pull this off, won't do anything to help the situation. Or my disposition, for that matter," she added with a small laugh. "There's no sense in analyzing my situation to death."

"You must admit you make an interesting character study. One doesn't normally stumble across such loyalty and determination in the average boatyard."

"Brewster's is only that—the average boat-yard."

"Maybe. But the owner is as far from average as one woman is likely to get."

He waited for Teak to look at him. Her eyes were wide, curious, full to brimming with a warmth that challenged the embers dropping silently on the hearth beside them. "Flattery," she murmured.

"Honest appraisal. An accurate observation."

"You're very good at that."

"I didn't mean to hurt you. If I went too far this afternoon, I'm sorry."

She concentrated on her meal.

Over the main course, Derek changed the subject. "You still haven't told me where I was the night you were partying in my kitchen."

Teak laughed. "I suppose there are lots of options."

"Give me a hint."

"It was close to midnight. The town pier. Flashing blue lights."

He groaned. "You must mean the night I got arrested for stripping and skinny-dipping at the town landing."

"Your father answered the phone. We were stirring cocoa, which began to simmer about the same time he did. 'Naked as a jaybird' was the way he described you."

"It was a dare. There were four of us." He sighed. "In those days everything was a dare. Anything to stir up a little excitement."

"To get someone to pay attention?"

He shrugged. "Water over the dam. I was never above livening things up. I spent all my time complaining about how dead this place was in the summer."

"And now you intend to tough it out for the winter?"

"I'm not that kid any longer. I can make a difference in your boatyard." His pause was almost imperceptible. "Whether or not you keep it."

"I told you what I, what the boatyard, stands to lose if you stay as fickle as you have been."

"I give you my word that I won't jump ship. Draw up a contract, if that'll make you feel better. You have nothing to lose, everything to gain." His smile was pure sensuality and he knew it.

"I want references. I'm serious about wanting to see some sort of portfolio of your work. *If* you wind up renting my shed, our relationship has to remain purely professional."

"Teresa Brewster, you have a one-track mind."

"And you don't? Self-preservation runs deep in my family."

"Take me on. Say yes."

"When was the last time anyone said no to you?"

The question brought him up short. He ate.

"That long ago?" She murmured it as she waited.

Derek looked at Teak over his fork. "Be careful what you ask. The answers may surprise you."

"I'm serious, Derek. The world's been at your feet all your life. It makes career switches and shop moves painless."

"It hasn't been painless." He lowered his fork to his plate. Teak swallowed the last of her wine. She had a thin gold chain around her neck, and he watched it rise and fall softly as she breathed.

She focused on some spot over his shoulder, then she glanced at him. "How much of the pain is connected to the partly carved shell on the footboard of your bed?"

Nine

The waiter appeared at Derek's shoulder. "Dessert?"

"Nothing, just the—"

"I'll have Indian pudding and herbal tea," Teak said.

"Orange spice, Zest . . ."

"The spice, please."

The waiter looked at Derek. "Nothing for you?"

Teak smiled at him. "You really can't leave the Winsor without having their Indian pudding. People drive down from—"

Derek cut her off. "I'll have a brandy and a second spoon."

Teak looked at Derek's self-satisfied expression. He radiated confidence, expectation . . . and sensuality, far too much sensuality. When the waiter left, Derek glared at her. "Indian pudding after that meal?"

She smiled. "You eat it in nibbles. I need an excuse to keep you where you are a little longer."

"Keep me here?"

"Until you answer my question." She waited as he scowled.

"Teak, you're self-reliant, independent and I'm sure you're used to running your own show, but you can't just cut to the bone every time we have a conversation." The pudding and tea arrived. A snifter of brandy and a spoon were placed in front of Derek.

She puckered and blew at the steam rising from her teacup. "Why not? You cut me to ribbons this afternoon, and I'm still here."

"I'd love to hear a few reasons."

"Oh, no, you don't. We were talking about you, not me."

"In a minute. Tell me why you're here."

"Because I'm resigned to admitting you might be a business risk worth taking. You certainly go right for what you're after. A woman can't?"

"You're not just any woman."

"Goodness."

"I know what I'm after." He sipped his brandy.

She wagged her finger. "Which is why we're here and not in your kitchen."

He smiled ruefully. "What I'm after in my professional life, Teak. Things are not as random and impetuous as they appear. You have only the vaguest idea of who I am."

"My vague ideas have set the wheels in motion. That's why I ordered dessert."

"You're expecting the rest of my life story over your Indian pudding?"

"You want me to hire you. You want your workshop in my shed and your reputation tied up with my boatyard's. Yes, I'm waiting for your life story. Some conversation over dessert is a logical place to start."

"I've already told you most of it."

"All these years I've known as much about you as you want the world to know. I'm beginning to see that underneath all that mystique and intrigue lies somebody else. You can't blame me for wondering who he is." She took a bite with her heart pounding, and watched the amber liquid as Derek swirled his brandy and drank.

He closed his eyes as he swallowed. "There's nothing you need to know except I've made major changes in my career and my life. None of that would even be relevant except that you know my family background."

"Knowing something about who you are helps explain the rest."

"Helps you, maybe."

"Who didn't it help?"

Derek shook his head. "You're right about how different we are. Bud Brewster opened the world to you. With his blessing off you went, free to stumble along your own path, free to make mistakes. Free to recreate yourself in a city where no one knows you. Free to succeed. You weren't following in anybody's footsteps. I had a private education. I went to my father's prep schools, joined my brother's fraternity. I followed my cousins, my mother, father and grandfather to Cornell. Of course the next step was to follow my brother and father to Tate Electronics."

"Which you did."

"Gave it my best shot. I hope you believe that. I was responsible and hardworking, if not dedicated. It was never what I wanted, even with the promotions and the money. I've always been good with my hands, loved building, creating, designing. We... I...was living in Connecticut and I met Davies. One thing led to another. I was smart enough to recognize that what I called my weekend hobby was keeping me sane. The woodworking was my only source of pleasure. The decision to leave

Tate was hard. The decision to tell them what I planned to do instead was excruciating.''

Derek's gaze drifted from her to his glass and back. Teak ate some of the pudding. "I suppose your beautiful hand-crafted bed fits into this somehow?''

"The damned bed. I angered a lot of people. Hurt them on purpose, they'd tell you. My father, for one.''

Teak brushed his fingers and took the snifter. A swallow of the liquor burned its way into her stomach. Fortitude. "It wasn't his initials you started to carve.''

"No.''

She took another swallow and waited.

"They were a woman named Hilary's.'' He reached for the glass and drained the last of the brandy, then signaled for the check. "HDT. Hilary Donahue.''

Teak finished her pudding, aching for Derek to break the silence. He didn't. "Hilary Donahue Tate?''

"Nearly.'' He glanced at the fire.

"Until you decided to give up reality for dreams, electronics for carpentry?'' Teak tried to read his expression. The idea that someone might have trampled this man's heart was incongruous. It didn't fit her version of the impenetrable Derek Tate any more than the rest of what she'd learned about him. Teak's heart ached as she scanned his face for signs of pain. His eyes were full of regret.

"Were you together long?"

"Quite a while."

"Engaged? Surely I would have read it in the *Times,* or heard the Skerrystead scuttlebutt."

"We had an understanding."

"I'm sorry."

"So am I." His tone stabbed her. "You weren't meant to snoop over the footboard when you used the bathroom in Wellfleet."

"It was an honest mistake. I was admiring the design." Help me out, she wanted to plead. One look at him told her he wouldn't. Derek paid the waiter, stood up and waited for her. He opened his hand over her back and the heat pressed through the lamb's wool. They walked to the parking lot in silence.

She'd pried her way too far into his personal life. Intriguing as it was, Teak was uncomfortable with the intimacy it implied, as well as the pain it had produced.

The night was crisp, just short of cold. Pumpkins and cornstalks decorated the walkway and lampposts to the parking lot. Their breath came in frosty smoke. They stopped at her truck and she lightened her tone. "So you've gone on with your life? New career, new addresses, new clients."

"Yes. No headaches. No stress attacks, no ulcers."

"If Hilary could see you now."

"You've asked about the bed and I gave you your answers. Let's leave Hilary out of things from now on."

"You're right. I'm sorry. I've probably gone too far tonight, but you should understand that you've always seemed so—I don't know—beyond emotion, above heartbreak. I guess I'm relieved to find out that you're human like the rest of us."

Teak shivered and Derek put his hands on her shoulders. "I was always human. I just don't like too many people to know. Ruins my image."

"I suppose Hilary broke everything off when she realized you were serious about leaving the firm and changing what amounted to her future?"

"Hilary? Hell, no. That would have made it all bearable. You've got it backward. I was the unforgiven. I was the one who broke off everything."

"You?"

"I broke it off the night before the engagement."

It wasn't the first time Derek had held his wild card until the last moment in some unconscious attempt to pull back from where Teak Brewster was taking him. For three weeks desire had teased him. For hours this...whatever the hell it was...had been smothering him in something dangerously close to contentment. Both were emotions dead to him for too long. Teak had cajoled, hinted, sighed and listened. The compassion and wonder in her expression were as compelling and unnerving as the honey in her voice. Guilt washed through him, tightening his chest as her expression changed to shock.

"Always the heartbreaker," Teak managed.

"I made her miserable."

"I think I've pried enough out of you for one night. Your personal life is your own."

"A little late for that, isn't it?"

"You were the one who warned me about asking questions."

"You're very good at giving the impression that you know the answers before you ask. It's tough to discover that's not always the case."

Teak trembled under his hands and flushed, even in the cold. "Thank you for dinner."

"My pleasure." He ran his hands along her sweatered arms and drew her to him. "I know you find it hard to believe, but it isn't just physical pleasure I find with you. It isn't just *my* pleasure I think about, either." When she didn't resist, he opened himself to the sensation of her warmth. She slid her arms under his sports jacket, across his back and when he kissed her, her mouth was warm, moist. She tasted faintly of spiced tea and nutmeg.

He lost himself in the response of his own body. Kissing Teak was like gulping air after too long in the depths of a black pool. "Brandy," she murmured.

"For warming a body up on a chilly night, you're better than a shot of the best."

She laughed into his jaw, nuzzled it briefly and drew back. "I'm due at the yard at seven."

"We could fill all those hours in between."

"Good night, Derek."

"I'll see you in the morning."

"With portfolio in hand."

"The Bendettes bought *Kestral*." At eight-thirty the following morning, Derek leaned across Teak's desk and gave her the news.

"You're forcing my hand."

"I'm bringing you customers, cash in hand. In addition to their assumption that Brewster Boatyard can haul, store and repair their boat, Paul and Bay happened to mention having already recommended us to another wooden boat owner in Alden's Cove."

Us. There it was again.

"As promised," he added as he laid his portfolio on her desk.

Teak unzipped the leather case and began to flip slowly through a collection of professionally arranged photographs. The first section was of bookshelves, an entertainment center and a corner cupboard, each obviously in a home or office. The next section consisted of individual pieces of furniture. The first was a Chippendale kneehole desk, a block-front chest, then a tea table. A set of contemporary chairs finished the grouping.

He watched as she ran her fingers lightly over the protective plastic pockets as if she could stroke the soft woods. "Derek, I had no idea. These are exquisite."

"Finely crafted, I like to say."

"Are these all custom pieces?"

"Mostly. A few are in a shop in New York where I've done most of my business."

"Long haul from Wellfleet."

"The distance keeps me sane."

"So you keep telling me. All right, set up shop."

He shook her hand. She smelled faintly— nicely—of cologne. One side of her collar poked from her cable-knit sweater and he had to fight the urge to adjust the other side. "It'll be in working order by tomorrow."

Teak swiveled in her chair. "I'm still putting you on a trial basis. If everything works out between us..." She caught his grin. "Between you and the yard, I want you to sign a two-year contract."

"What if you find buyers who want to bring in their own wooden boat setup?"

"If that happens, we'll make it part of the negotiations."

"*We.* I like the sound of that," Derek replied.

Teak glanced at him, then concentrated on her morning coffee." You won't last two weeks unless you knock off the innuendo."

"A lot can happen in two weeks."

"Don't you have a workbench to install, or chisels to unpack?"

"Certainly." He took her hand and shook it firmly. "Whatever else happens, you won't regret this partnership, Teak." Whatever else happens. What in the name of saws and wood lathes *was* happening?

He sauntered across the parking lot in the direction of his car. As he broke from the shade of the building, the sunlight streamed down on him. He couldn't hold a conversation with her without his adrenaline going haywire.

He couldn't discuss business without thinking of how she'd looked across the dining table at the Winsor Inn. Worst of all, he couldn't look at her without remembering every ridiculous, simmering, tremulous, breathtaking response she'd had to his kiss. Kisses, to be more accurate. The woman had a way with kisses that left him aching for more. It was an ache impossible to ignore.

Ten

Manny Souza and the machine shop kept Teak occupied until noon. There was a misplaced order for parts and an error in the shop inventory, which, even with the computerized system, took the two of them the rest of the morning to straighten out.

"Computers ain't my thing, especially when they're wrong," he kept muttering over her shoulder as they checked and double-checked what he swore was not in the stockroom, but the computer screen kept verifying.

"It's human error, Manny."

"Well, some human's used up the last of the

motor oil without marking it down." He poked the screen with his finger. "Type that in, right there. Commercial grade engine oil. I'll pick up a case in Hyannis tomorrow."

"Thanks. Have you taken a look at Derek's engine yet?"

"My next project. Yours seems to be adding wooden boat repair and carpentry to the yard."

Teak flushed. "You've talked to Derek?"

"Would have rather heard it from you. Fine idea, if you ask me. Of course nobody did."

She patted his arm. "The truth is, it was Derek's idea. He sort of sprung it on me after the *Kestral* was sold and the owners came in search of somebody to repair it."

"Derek reliable these days? Have you checked any references?" Her flush deepened and Manny wagged a finger. "You just keep your eyes wide open with this one."

"Of course! This is all business. His portfolio is first-rate. He'll bring in work. While we're on the subject, I need your opinion. I want us to bid on the Skerrystead Yacht Club account. You're already working on their launch boat's engine. They've used Harbor Street Marina since the beginning of time and it's my understanding that the relationship's gone stale.

"We've got the equipment and the manpower to manage the float and docks. We've been pulling and setting independent moorings since Pop's been in business. So why not private clubs, too?''

''I say go for it.''

''I knew you would. I'll try to set up an appointment midweek with the club manager and somebody from their executive committee.''

''Maybe you are a chip off your old man. He'd a gone after anything it took to keep this afloat.''

''Was there a compliment in there somewhere?''

Manny squinted at her. ''You know me better than that.''

Teak waved him off and put her palm to her overheated cheek. Derek Tate had to remain business as usual. He was no different than any other new account. Whatever was brewing between herself and the wooden boat expert would be misconstrued at the least and shared with every male in the yard at the most. She shuddered at the thought.

Greg arrived with the Bendettes' boat at two that afternoon. She and Derek walked the huge shed doors back on their tracks and watched as the *Kestral* disappeared into the cavernous space.

Derek rubbed his hands together. ''This is a project I'm going to enjoy.''

''How long did you give the family business a try?''

''Too long.''

''That bad?''

"It wasn't all bad, of course. I thought marketing was what I wanted. I started in the manufacturing center outside Chicago and finished at the home office."

"Manhattan?"

"Worked in Midtown. Lived out in Darien."

"With Hilary."

"In close proximity to Hilary. All the while you were down in the financial district."

"Small world, Derek."

His glance took in the boatyard. "Getting smaller all the time."

In the three days since he'd started the repairs on *Kestral,* Derek began to feel accepted by the men in the yard. Even those who'd known him as the spoiled son of one of the yard's wealthiest customers wandered in on their coffee breaks to check on his progress or swap boat stories. They offered tools and unsolicited advice, and if they'd expected pretense or aloofness, they were pleasantly mistaken. The one exception was his boss. Teak's restlessness seem to grow in direct proportion to his acceptance. On Wednesday morning she appeared at the door with a delivery. As usual she was in her jeans and a cotton sweater, green this time, with flecks of yellow. Being within fifty yards of her was invigorating. Within ten, and he was conscious of every fiber of his body.

"Your fastenings have arrived."

Derek rubbed his sleeve across his forehead. "Come on in."

She put the carton on the workbench and glanced at the mechanical drawings and sketches of a mirror that he'd tacked to the bulletin board. "Next project?"

"A client and I designed a mirror to match a table I made for her about a year ago."

"This looks beautiful." She traced the inverted shell on the graph paper. "Mahogany?"

"With gilt. There's a firm I use in Boston for that."

Teak was quiet. He watched her turn. Her boat shoe left an imprint in the sawdust as she crossed the cement floor to the boat. She made a pretense of looking at *Kestral*'s stern post. If she felt his stare, she gave no indication. It surprised him how much pleasure he got from simply watching her move.

Derek got back to work. "Anything I can do for you?"

"Keeping this shed busy is enough for now."

"Happy to oblige."

"You are, aren't you? Happy, I mean."

"Damned happy, if you want the truth. It hasn't been easy getting to this point. Even you still have doubts about me."

"You must admit—"

"That Derek Tate belongs back in a pin-striped suit with a suite of offices?"

"Yes, maybe."

"Or is it that I'm not living up to my reputation? Admit it, Teak. You're still half expecting me to pull in here about noon, maybe a little hung over, full of plans for the night."

"It wouldn't have surprised me at first."

"And now?"

"I expect you to live up to the reputation *you've* described."

"I intend to. I think half the crew around here feels the same way as you do, though."

"Maybe the first day. I've never seen anybody accepted so fast."

"Frustrating, isn't it?"

She leaned against the boat and looked at him. "Yes, if you want the truth. Why should I deny it? None of the men, not even Manny, knows quite what to make of me. Every one of them holds me at arm's length, doubts my expertise, questions my authority. You arrive, and it's one big coffee break."

"Look at it from their point of view. You're the kid they watched grow up. You're Bud's daughter. You left all dewy-eyed and college bound and came back all business and common sense."

"That's what the yard needs."

"There's more."

"What more could there be? They resent working for a woman, they want a man in that office."

Derek chuckled. "It's not resentment. It's closer to fear."

"Fear!"

"Down to a man they respect you. It's just that you're young and great-looking and they're walking on eggs to keep from having any comment or gesture be misconstrued."

"Misconstrued."

"Sexual harassment. If you had a husband and kids hanging around—"

"Just one blasted minute."

"You've told me yourself you want them."

"Eventually."

"I just meant, if you were married, it would take the edge off a little. These things aren't insurmountable, they just take time. Give the guys a chance to get comfortable with you. You've broken their routine, invaded their space."

"Pop psychology."

"Just my opinion."

"I doubt that. Obviously they talk to you about me." She gritted her teeth. "Do they all huddle in here over their coffee and chew me to pieces?"

"I told you they respect you. They respect Bud."

"So they behave for my father's sake."

Derek grinned. "That may be part of it. It wouldn't hurt you to join us. Come on in with a cup of coffee when you see them taking a break. Chew the fat. Let them see you can be one of the boys.''

''The perfect blend of management and labor.''

''It's a boatyard, Teak, not a firm of pencil-pushing CPAs. Loosen up. Hang out with them, in spirit, anyway. They know you went to college. Hell, your old man bragged about you day and night. They know you're back here because you have to be, all rich and famous and self-sacrificing.''

''Derek, I am not—''

''They respect you for what you're doing. Just don't...'' He shrugged in midsentence and stepped over to the box she'd brought him. Opening it gave him something to concentrate on besides the waves of desire threatening to shred his common sense.

She stepped beside him, so close he caught the trace of cologne again. ''What were you going to add?''

''You're making it obvious that I've said enough.''

''You might as well finish.''

''I was going to say that the grease won't rub off. They are what they are.''

''And?''

''And you are what you've chosen to become.''

''Am I supposed to apologize?''

''That's not the point,'' Derek said.

Her cheeks flamed, but it was impossible to tell whether it was from anger or embarrassment. Derek ran his fingertips over the bridge of her nose and down along her jaw. "A cup of coffee with them now and then, a little idle conversation won't dissolve all those years and miles you've put between yourself and your roots. The men in this yard aren't after anything more than continued financial security and job guarantees."

Teak put her hand over his wrist and slowly pulled his hand from her face. "You've said just about enough."

"Have I? It's your welfare I have at heart, Teak, your boatyard. And one last thing. There's not a man among them who would blame me for aching to kiss you again."

"Sexual harassment," she murmured as his mouth grazed hers.

"Desire, Teresa Brewster, pure and simple."

Eleven

Pure, maybe, but there was nothing simple about Teak's reaction. She leaned against him and felt him support her at the small of her back. His hand was under her sweater, warm, wide over her spine, pressing her perfectly against the length of him. He shifted his thighs, and the heat swirled.

They could have danced, they could have swayed, they could have sunk together to the sawdust and made love for long, stolen moments. Anything was possible in this man's arms.

Teak returned his kisses. Her fingers brushed his sweater, played in his hair. He moaned softly as she touched his cheek. He held her against him and she moved gently from side to side until she was molded, breasts to hips, to his contours. ''Perfect,'' he groaned.

Oh, to be reckless! The rush of desire continued to build, as if her body were pulling the energy from his, only to return it tenfold. Derek left no doubt that he would take her as far as she'd dare. The boy of her adolescent dreams, the guy who had made her feel this way since the day she'd first laid eyes on him, wanted her, ached to kiss her! For one long, intoxicating moment, she let herself race, right smack to the limit of her self-control, not one step farther.

Even as she kissed him, even as she reveled in the pleasure, she thought about the men she supervised. Teak Brewster had spent a lifetime in the yard, long enough to know what back-room gossip was, how often it centered around women, how fast it traveled, how much damage it could do. Wouldn't they love a few hints from Derek about this?

No doubt they'd already pressed him for something. Under the sandpaper exterior, Manny Souza was the patron saint of righteousness when it came to her well-being. The rest of them, however, would love nothing more than some spicy speculation to chew on. That knowledge alone was enough to keep herself in check in Derek's arms. Let him ache.

Weak knees, flailing heart and a body that was already filling every nook and cranny of his made the separation tougher than she'd anticipated. She sighed over one last kiss and planted her hands against his chest. Derek's breathing was as erratic as hers.

"Teak, do you have any idea how much I want—"

She put her fingers against his lips. "If you really have my welfare at heart, you'll take no for an answer. This is fun, but it's reckless."

"Reckless doesn't begin to describe what we have together."

She looked into his eyes. "There's too much at stake for me to give in to what's nothing more than physical desire."

"You might enjoy yourself."

She ran a finger over his bottom lip. "I don't doubt that for a minute."

Derek's gaze widened. Surprise and remnants of desire darkened them as he smiled. "Oh, darlin'."

"There are five men employed in the boatyard, all of whom spend an inordinate amount of time contemplating their respective relationships with me. You've just spent ten minutes telling me what they really think. This is a trial period for all of us, you included."

"I can handle both."

"Maybe, maybe not. I would have to be a complete nitwit to jeopardize what's already tough enough. Jumping into bed with you would be professional suicide."

"Jumping into bed with me would be the most pleasurable way to go."

"Derek, I'm serious."

"So am I. Stop beating your beautiful breasts over professional suicide." He raised his hands and traced their outline with his thumbs. Instantly desire returned. She arched and closed her eyes against the flush and the raw passion in Derek's eyes. Teak moved his hands.

"We can keep this separate," he groaned.

"Not in this atmosphere."

"We're adults, Teak. I've grown beyond sharing gossip in the locker room. Don't you think I care about your reputation?"

"You're as naive as you are desirable. You've worked in an office, surely you must have noticed an illicit romance or two. Furtive glances, blushes, stolen kisses in the stairwell, it's all inevitable."

"Who was he?"

"Who was who?"

"The guy who got you in the stairwell. You sound so knowledgeable."

"You've missed the point entirely. It's not my reputation at stake, it's yours."

"Mine?"

"I've got yardmen who've known me all my life. If they so much as suspect you've been treating me—lightly—they'll come after you with truck jacks."

"It would be worth it."

She kissed him then, hard and quick on the mouth, enjoying his gasp of surprise. "I'm saving your hide. Get back to work, Derek, darling, before Manny or Greg suspect anything."

Get back to work. As if his breathing, his body or his psyche would let him. Derek stood next to *Kestral* for five long minutes staring at the shed door Teak had closed as she left him. Thirty years old, at loose ends all of his life, and now, when he'd finally found roots for that restlessness in something constructive, a woman was tying those ends in knots, knots no sailor ever imagined.

He turned reluctantly to the boat and tried to concentrate on the dead wood and stern post. He wound up pressing his forehead against the hull and running his hand slowly over the planking. "Teak Brewster," he whispered, "Come hell or high water..."

"She giving you trouble?"

Derek raised his head and turned to face Manny Souza, who was already halfway across the workshop. Derek cleared his throat and hoped it would appear that his problems were professional. "She's giving me a run for my money, I'll say that much."

"You got much experience at this sort of thing?"

"Lord, yes. At least I thought so. I'm not sure experience counts for much in this case. Teak's a woman unto herself and she'll run this yard the way she wants."

"Teak? I was talking about the boat, here, *Kestral.*" He narrowed his gaze. "Not that I haven't been giving this whole setup a lot of thought."

"Wooden boat repair's the perfect addition to the yard. It may take a while, but word of mouth and some decent advertising should bring in new revenue."

"Should." The mechanic looked over the tool bench and inspected the boat. "I hope that's the reason you're here."

Derek scuffed some sawdust. "None other."

"Wouldn't have nothing to do with the owner's daughter?"

"You were here when I first showed up. I was looking for Bud. I had no idea he'd died. I'm embarrassed to say I didn't even remember Teak." He neglected to add that the first visit had only been to arrange boat storage.

"Good." The men glanced at each other. Manny's voice was careworn. "If you're out to put your boss through hoops, give it up."

"Manny, you and I both know Teak Brewster can take care of herself just fine."

"That includes seeing to her own needs. You're none of my business, I know that, and I'm out of line telling you this." For all his years, the mechanic still looked uncomfortable. He ran his hand over the table saw before looking at Derek. "Still, there's part of me who still sees you as that wild teenager, shoplifting from Bud."

"Teak knows all about it."

"Forgives you, too. Tells you she understands, I bet. There were summers when Teak would have stood on her head to get your attention."

"She's already told me. We were kids, living different lives."

"You were grown, in college—twenty, twenty-one—the year you cracked up your old man's powerboat. She was all of seventeen, eighteen. You'd storm in here every day, checking on the repairs, treating men old enough to be your father as if they were at your beck and call. None of us could patch it fast enough for your liking."

"There's a lot I regret about those years."

"Teak even shared her lunch with you a couple of times, tried to flirt a little."

"I don't remember, Manny. To be honest, I wish I didn't remember most of those years, but I'm not that spoiled kid any longer."

"There's a point here, Derek."

"Then make it."

"I didn't like you then. I'm hoping I'll see a reason to change my mind. Teak's hired you and stuck you out here in this shed. She must be convinced you'll bring in revenue. Must be convinced you mean to stick to something. Don't go messing things up."

The men sized each other up. Derek sighed. "Don't confuse me with the headstrong, self-centered kid I used to be. Teak and I've agreed to a trial run with this shop. You ought to be able to live with that, too."

Manny seemed to soften. "She says she sees a good thing for the yard."

"She does."

The mechanic sighed. "Teak's not that moon-struck teenager anymore. The Brewster women aren't your type."

"Thanks for the advice."

"Take it. Teak don't make time for carpenters. Her heart's not here, anyway. I'm sure she told you the plan for the yard."

"She told me."

"Then we understand each other?"

"I understand that you think you need to protect her. She's an independent woman, Manny, one whose been making her own decisions for a long time. She's an excellent judge of character with a good business sense. I'm not sure she needs all this

concern." He looked from the boat to the mechanic. "But she's lucky to have it."

"I'm looking out for Bud's best interest, too."

"According to Teak he encouraged all of his
daughters."

"He did. Teak's the only one left of the bunch,
the only one who didn't follow the plan. Bud
stewed about it something awful, her being single
in New York."

"Wasn't she ever involved with anybody?"

"She'd get this fellow or that one in her life, but
nothing ever came of it, least nothing Bud ever
knew. She wouldn't bring them home. Never a visit
to Skerrystead. Course he blamed that on himself.
Always preaching to those girls to do better, find a
rich one's got some polish."

"The all-important polish."

Manny cocked his head. "Bud needed to understand when you're living that New York life and
you got a fellow all full of spit and polish, you don't
bring him home to the boatyard." He looked Derek over. "I suppose you do fit in that spit-and-
polish category, with your background and all. The
exception's this work you do."

Manny seemed visibly relaxed and Derek
searched for something to change the subject.
"How did Teak's sisters turn out? Did they both
take Bud's advice?"

"Dana's a psychologist, married to a doctor. Molly's teaching something or other, husband's an engineer of some sort." Manny crossed to the door. "I better get back to the shop, as long as we understand each other."

"If you come flying in here every time you suspect Teak's been by, she'll be looking for a new mechanic."

He flushed and poked at his collar. "I got this yard at heart, same as I got Bud's daughter there. Just make sure you remember that."

"I'm not likely to forget it."

Twelve

———

Teak left the boatyard at lunchtime relieved that she had something to concentrate on other than the carpenter and her jangling nerves. Half of her—a very dangerous half—was ticking like a clock. The moment she came within shouting distance of Derek, she found herself giving serious thought to his erotic invitations. Her second half, in full voice, brought her up short with a simple: What? Are you out of your mind?

She drove home and forced herself to shelve even the remotest thoughts of Derek Tate. For the moment, she had bigger fish to fry. Lunch was little more than nibbles of a salad in her kitchen as she planned her strategy.

The Brewster residence was a small, high-ceilinged farmhouse on the northern edge of Skerrystead. It looked out on the sand hills, flat rectangular cranberry bogs and piney woods where a good portion of Skerrystead's laborers earned their living. It was the patchwork of bogs that divided the town and separated what passed for a local year-round labor force from the summer residents who clung to the waterfront.

At the moment the area was at its most beautiful. It was the midst of the cranberry harvest, and the flooded bogs glistened with crimson berries. The maple and beech trees filled the landscape with golds and reds, like nothing she had seen on West Eighty-second Street.

The Brewster house had changed little since Teak and her sisters had breathed life into it. Assorted school portraits still sat on the mantel. Faded bedspreads covered the twin beds in the room she'd shared with Molly. When she'd first returned, her father's possessions made the house seem melancholy, but as her grief subsided, she found herself calmed by the security and happy memories the atmosphere possessed.

She changed into a simple linen skirt and pushed the sleeves of the matching navy jacket up to her elbows. The only splash of color was a bright pink

blouse cut below the throat and set off with a thin
gold chain. It was an ensemble she'd used numer-
ous times when she visited clients' accounting offices. Tasteful, appropriate, serious. She also
freshened her makeup. "Knock 'em dead," she said
in the mirror as she ran her fingers through her hair.

Before she left she put a call in to Dana, who'd
settled in Needham, west of Boston. She discussed
her yacht club plan with her sister, and the November Thanksgiving holiday, when all the Brewsters
planned to gather at the house.

Teak sighed. "It'll be tough without Pop."

"I suppose we'll need to talk about selling the
house, once you go back to New York."

"And dividing up the furniture. There's a lifetime of stuff still here, your old yearbook included."

"You do know how much Molly and I appreci-
ate what you're doing?"

"Of course."

"I suppose your social life's gone down the
tubes, too. Have you run into anybody single in
Skerrystead?"

"Dana, I'm much too busy with business."

They closed the conversation with trivia of the
yard and Manny Souza's disposition. As tempting
as it was, she made sure not to bring the name Derek Tate into the conversation. At best she could

expect teasing, at worst Dana might—as only a sister could—really try to dig for information.

As soon as she hung up the phone, she drove into the village, along the commercial end of Pilgrim Street and past the boatyard. The shops and offices that comprised the business district faced the Common with their backs to the water. Once past the town landing, the road became residential. Antique Capes and foursquare Georgian houses from the whaling days shared lanes with roomy summer places battened till spring or rented to local families until their owners returned.

Breaker's Point formed the peninsula at the end. Just before the bend that curved out to the exclusive address, there was an opening in a trim border of hedge roses. Skerrystead Yacht Club, Members Only was posted demurely at the curb.

Teak had five minutes to spare before the chairman of the executive committee and the club's hired manager had agreed to listen to her pitch on behalf of the boatyard. She bounced over the sandy lane and down to the waterfront clubhouse. The floats and docks were still in the water, but the private pleasure crafts and club boats for sailing classes had all been pulled for the winter. Because the club catered primarily to summer residents, activity was at a minimum. Two women were playing platform tennis in sweaters and sweatpants on the waterfront courts.

Teak had been on the grounds half a dozen times as a kid, accompanying Greg to haul one or another yacht up the launch ramp. However, her private invitations consisted of a single summer when the club opened its teenage dances to the public. Hoping Derek would be there, she'd come twice with her town friends. Both times she'd stood in the corner all night watching him and his fellow junior members share private jokes and adolescent behavior, then called it quits. Even then she knew her future lay outside the confines of this narrow social stratum.

With a sigh, she watched the sea gulls swoop and perch on the pier. At the appropriate time, she climbed the steps to the business offices.

"Miss Brewster? Teak?"

"Yes." She turned as a well-dressed man in his early thirties came onto the porch.

"I'm Brock Morrison, from the executive committee. The club manager's just inside. Come on in. We're anxious to hear your pitch."

Derek had taken to eating his lunch on the run. Most often, when he could spare the time, he sought out one of his favorite childhood haunts. Today his need to get out of the boatyard was critical. One more time he reprimanded himself. He had delicate work to think about. *Kestral* demanded his full attention. So, surprisingly, did his body. Something had to be done, and soon.

His adrenaline surged. His head ached. He was hard in places where he shouldn't be. He was soft where he should be sharp. The hell of it was the pleasure. This misery felt wonderful. He was enjoying every frustrating, tantalizing minute of this convoluted relationship. The chase was everything.

Teak Brewster's mystique kept his blood racing. Her reticence fired his imagination. Gorgeous package that she was, she also had a clear head for business, which he admired. If anyone could pull the boatyard together and make a profit, he sensed it would be her. The men would work with her, some because they had to, but most because she had the innate ability to garner their respect, treat them fairly and maintain the quality her father was known for. He could see those traits in her and he could see Skerrystead Boatyard providing a comfortable living under her direction.

Derek also sensed her wariness, her determination, and most of all the underlying sensuality that continually produced the volatile chemistry between them. The missing element, however, was time. Running back to New York so soon wouldn't do more than maintain the status quo at the boatyard. He suspected what competition there was for her attention had more to do with work than men.

If she was bound and determined to race back to Manhattan, so be it. Happily ever after, as his parents and Hilary Gates could attest, had never been part of his vocabulary.

He forced himself to clear his head and drove his car across the patch of pavement that led to the marshy waterline on the grounds of the yacht club. As a kid, he had launched countless boats there for the steady parade of sailing instructors who taught his classes. He got out and walked to the shoreline. The tide was high. He ate his sandwich as he watched the water sway the marsh grass and listened to the *thwack* of the paddle ball on the nearby court.

The autumn light was different from the intensity of July. Amber pools floated over the marsh, reflecting the brilliance of the foliage hanging over the shoreline. The hydrangeas and roses had faded, but the sugar maples and fire thorn hedges were bright. He knew the club grounds only as summer green. It was a welcome change. So far Skerrystead was full of welcome changes.

Midway through his sandwich he shuffled coins in his pocket and wondered if he could pick up a soft drink at the clubhouse dining room, dressed as he was. Derek started off toward the porch, flipping his quarters and dimes in his palm. He caught a glimpse of a pin-striped suit, designer shoes—Brock Morrison dressed to the nines. Out to impress somebody, he thought, as another of his Breaker's Point neighbors stepped onto the porch. Derek looked down at his money. The next time he glanced up, Teak Brewster was standing in the doorway.

At least he thought it was Teak. There was a streak of something soft and pink, vibrant against her throat, and a flash of great legs, no denim. Thin kid heels, that hair... The shock jump started his respiratory system. The ache in his chest was instant, as if she'd just pulled from one of his embraces. She was laughing at something Brock was saying and shaking his hand. After seeing her to the edge of the porch, Brock went inside.

Derek tightened his fist around the coins until they dug into his palm. A lunch date? Hadn't he heard that Brock was married again? Maybe it was that he'd been divorced again.

As he crossed the lawn, Teak turned and spotted him. He watched her face. Surprise arched her brows. She touched her hair, tapped her foot, waited as he arrived. "Hello, Derek."

"Lunch date?"

She looked at the doors. "With Brock?"

"Brock Morrison. How the heck do you know him?"

"The same way I know you. He's kept his boats at our yard for years. How do *you* know him?"

"He's a neighbor. The club. I've known Morrison and his string of wives all my life."

"He's single."

"Again," Derek muttered. "He lives out on the Point year-round."

"I know." She started across the porch and he could see now that her truck was parked at the edge of the small lot. It was next to Brock's German import. "Did you know he looked into buying *Kestral?*"

"Really. That's why you're out here, like that?"

She smiled. "Like what?"

"In this non-boatyard stuff."

Teak patted his arm and moved past him. "I don't always wear jeans. See you tomorrow."

"That's it?" He caught up to her.

"That's what?"

"That's all the explanation I'm going to get?"

"Why do I owe you an explanation?"

Derek sighed. "Forgive my curiosity but I leave you in the boatyard in sweaters and sawdust, having nearly made love to you standing up against my workbench. I go out to lunch to clear my head and find you dressed to kill, on my yacht club porch, laughing and holding hands with a guy who goes through women like I go through plywood."

Teak's complexion glowed. "I was shaking his hand, not holding it. We were sealing a business agreement.'' She looked down. ''Am I dressed to kill?''

''Compared to your usual getups. What was this, your version of a Skerrystead power lunch.''

''No lunch. *Your* club's restaurant is closed for the season.'' As he winced at her emphasis, she reached her truck and hoisted herself up, not altogether modestly. ''I'll see you tomorrow.''

''You're not going back to the yard?''

''Dressed like this? No. I'm meeting Brock again in an hour.'' She turned over the engine. He got the feeling she'd have backed over his work boots if he hadn't stepped aside.

''I don't know what the heck you're up to, but watch out for that guy.''

''Amazing. I mentioned that you were working out of my boatyard and he said the same thing about you.''

Thirteen

The following morning Teak sipped her coffee and munched on bagel as she walked to the boatyard's tidal inlet, where lobsterman Hank Maroney was unloading his traps from the stern of *Mary Beth*. The wind was up and rain was threatening.

She paid little attention to any of it. Her thoughts were still on Derek and his unexpected reaction to her the previous afternoon. She was trying to decide if she should be flattered or annoyed by his behavior. She'd had nearly nineteen hours to come to a conclusion, if she counted the hours he was part of her dreams and her insomnia. She was trying not to count. She was trying to concentrate on the business at hand, with very little luck.

Dismiss it, she kept telling herself. As she rounded the sheds, she settled on flattered. Derek Tate hardly seemed the type for a jealous streak. Jealous of whom, for that matter? She doubted any women had ever turned him down for anything.

Unconsciously she glanced at his shed and the empty space where she expected his car to arrive momentarily. There was something disconcerting about a man who had the ability to change careers, addresses, life-styles and companions whenever the mood struck. With the exception of Hilary Gates, they hadn't actually discussed companions, but there was no reason for that category of Derek's life to be any different from the rest.

Derek Tate got what he wanted. When he grew bored, he focused on something—or someone— else. Everything from his return from Wellfleet to the story behind the bed illustrated that. She thought about Hilary, tried to imagine the kind of woman Derek had come close to marrying, and what made him break it off within weeks of the marriage. Had Teak gotten wind of the story as Skerrystead rumor, she would have filed it away as typical behavior. Hearing it from Derek, watching his expression and listening to his voice was as unsettling as the man himself.

There was no denying that his attention was flattering, but she'd matured in the years away from Skerrystead, matured enough to recognize his interest in her for what it was, another conquest, another diversion to keep his restlessness and boredom at bay.

Teak was no neophyte when it came to men. If he found her intriguing, surely it was the mystique. For all Derek knew she had a string of ex-husbands and passionate lovers lying in the wake she'd left in New York. Why not? Perhaps he was banking on the chemistry between them. With a little work she could be as much of a femme fatale as the next woman. If Derek Tate was what she was after, maybe she should work on her style. The uninvited thought was such a surprise she stopped walking.

Rain began to splatter her foul-weather jacket and she pulled the hood up. She was not after Derek Tate. No detours, no sidetracks. She—and he— knew what her goal was. "And landing the yacht club account will get me one step closer. Business," she muttered. "Keep your head clear." Brewster Boatyard was not going to survive on idiotic daydreams and sexual fantasies, and neither would she.

Her reverie was interrupted by the sound of her name. Brock Morrison inched his car up next to her and let the engine idle. "Good morning. I drove over to give you some good news. Climb in out of the rain." He opened the passenger door.

Teak wiped at her jacket and thanked him as she slid in beside him. "Would you like to come back to my office?"

Brock shook his head. "No, I'm on my way to work. I just wanted to tell you in person that the club manager agrees with me. Your bid looked good. Frankly, the timing's perfect. The yard we've been using has slipped considerably in the past few years. The club's ready for some new blood." He smiled. "I guess you're the one. We'd like to give you a try."

Teak shook Brock's hand across the gearshift. "You won't regret it." They sat together for another ten minutes and discussed the hauling and setting of the docks and floats, and most importantly, the tune-up and overhaul of the engines of the yacht club fleet of launches and motorboats.

Brock watched the windshield wipers, then turned to Teak. "Would you consider closing the deal over dinner tonight?"

"Thanks, Brock, but I don't think so."

"Lunch?"

Derek's sports car made a sudden appearance at the entrance of the yard. Unconsciously, she turned and watched as it passed them and arced into the spot in front of his shed.

Brock laughed good-naturedly. "I should know better than to compete with Derek. You can't blame a guy for trying."

Teak turned to Brock. "Compete?"

"He made it clear after you left yesterday that you two are—"

"The two of you spoke about me?"

"Can't blame us."

"Derek's my employee."

"He said the two of you have an understanding."

"What, exactly, did he tell you the two of us understand?" This time she glared through the windshield.

"Teak, I don't want to make trouble for the two of you."

She opened the door. "Why don't I meet you at the Winsor Inn after work."

"Really?"

"About six-thirty."

As Brock agreed, Teak let herself out of the car and waved him off. The rain had settled into a steady drizzle. She should have been elated at winning the yacht club account, dancing on air, whooping for joy. Instead she scowled at the now-open shed door and ignored the hum of Derek's band saw. Dinner in some romantic setting with Brock Morrison had no appeal whatsoever. Nevertheless, she was just mad enough to do it.

* * *

Derek left the band saw running, but stayed a good fifteen feet away from it. The view from his open shed door had him far too distracted to risk using the dangerous piece of equipment. Electric saws demanded full attention, clear heads, concentration. The yellow blur of foul-weather gear on the passenger side behind the windshield of Brock Morrison's pretentious car commanded all of his.

What the hell was Teak doing letting him drive her to work? They were parked right in the middle of the yard, at eight o'clock in the morning! This wasn't the impersonal office of a megasize Wall Street CPA firm.

He snapped off the saw and waited. Teak got out and waved at the departing car. She turned, sipping coffee as if it was the most natural thing in the world. She chewed a bagel. A bagel! Above him the rain pelted on the metal roof. Derek growled.

She passed the open shed door without a sideways glance and by the time Derek had pulled on his slicker, there was no sight of her. He stepped into the lot and squinted as the rain began in earnest. It blew in sheets, driven by the wind off the water, and flattened his hair, soaked his face. He finally spotted a yellow blur on the pier at the edge of the inlet.

He caught up to her as she stepped aboard the *Mary Beth*. She and the lobsterman huddled in the wheelhouse, out of the elements, and Derek slowed

his pace. The force that had driven him after her
dissipated, and he realized as he stood there being
plummeted by the downpour that he had no reason for following her. He couldn't even put a name
to what had propelled him in the first place. Soaked
and disgusted with himself, he turned back to his
workshop. It was a long time before he turned on
the band saw.

He broke for lunch at one when Hank Maroney
came into the shed to borrow a pair of pliers.
"Manny Souza's good as they come when it comes
to engines, but John Kempski, the guy he's got
working for him is more trouble than he's worth.
This is the second time I've had to push the guy to
get to my engine. Simple request, and it's not as if
the yard's got boats lined up waiting."

"Have you mentioned it to Teak?"

"This morning I finally did. Her old man was
none too fond of him. Strung him along out of
kindness, I guess. He'll lose the yard customers is
what I told Teak."

"Did she listen?"

"Sure she listened. There's no margin to fool
around with these days. Hell of it is, I could do the
work myself off-season. And for what I pay this
yard, I'd save something in the long run."

"What if you paid less rent but had access to the
machine shop?"

"There's half a dozen of us who'd use it."

"Half a dozen renting somewhere else?"

"Mostly." He gave Derek a long look. "You seem to get on with her. Bring it up yourself. Twice in one day might do some good."

"Might." Might, indeed. Within the hour he was heading across the lot in the still-driving rain.

Teak's office door was closed and the nearest salesman advised Derek to wait. "She's attending to some unpleasant business. Shouldn't take too long."

Derek busied himself studying the display of signal flags and turned only when the door opened. John Kempski kept his hand on the doorknob.

"One more thing," he growled. "Bud'd never handle things this way."

Teak's answer was muffled.

"I knew you'd be trouble. No way a broad can run a yard. You'll sink it faster than a two-ton anchor."

"That's enough, John." Teak's voice came from the room's interior.

"You've been a pain in the butt since the morning you got here, getting in my way, giving me orders..."

"Getting a day's work out of you," she replied as she appeared at the door. "I'm sorry you have a problem with my position, but—"

"There's only one position your type's good for."

Derek made it to John in three swift strides. "Kempski, that's about enough."

The mechanic turned. "And you'd know what the position is, Tate."

Derek buried the impulse to punch. Instead he grabbed John by his arms, felt the biceps flex and wrapped his other hand around his back.

"This isn't your fight," John muttered.

From behind him Teak was protesting, but Derek managed to usher the mechanic to the front door, knocking life jackets onto the floor as he bumped the shelves. "If you don't want interference, then you don't continue your discussions in front of other people, Kempski."

When they got to the front step, John shook off Derek's grasp with a string of obscenities. "Forget it. I'm glad to be out of here. No way I'm working for that—"

"Kempski."

"All right, all right." He turned and marched into the rain. When Derek turned around, Teak was still in the doorway, flushed and tight lipped. He picked up the scattered flotation devices as he crossed the shop and went to her, chest heaving.

Her glance was icy. "I suppose you expect me to thank you."

"Hadn't given it much thought."

"Obviously. Just once I'd like a man to lead with his brain instead of his testosterone."

"Teak—"

She yanked him into the office and closed the door. "It was all for show, Derek. John got puffed up like a rooster when I criticized his work, but it wasn't anything I couldn't handle. There wasn't an obscenity till he opened the door. It was all for the benefit of you men out there waiting to turn this into a barroom brawl."

"He was insulting you."

"You're right. He was angry and embarrassed and that was his way of dealing with it. I don't like it, but that kind of behavior goes with the territory sometimes."

"You don't need it."

"Rough talk and I aren't strangers to each other. Blue language and sexist behavior have been around this yard longer than I have. If I hadn't thought I could handle it, I never would have come back here, even for this short period."

"Don't give the men fuel for the fire."

"What fuel?"

"It doesn't help your reputation any when you glide into an all-male boatyard at eight in the morning in the passenger seat of a forty-thousand-dollar car."

"Just any forty-thousand-dollar car?"

"In this case, no."

"Are you concerned about the car, or the driver?"

"You know what I mean."

"I know what you're implying."

"There's a double standard in places like this."

"With your attitude it won't change, either. Still, thanks for the advice. I'll remember never to do it." She stepped past him and out into the showroom as the salesman called her over to the front desk.

Fourteen

———

Teak bent between the narrow aisles and picked up the last of the life jackets. She stood up hugging two to her breasts, and came toe to toe with Derek. "You're still here."

"I came over to make a point."

"You've made enough points in the past few days to last till I go back to New York, thank you."

"It's a point that doesn't involve my testosterone."

"How refreshing."

"Teak Brewster, telephone," came over the yard's intercom system.

Derek swore. "It's a business proposition."

"I have to get the phone first. Be patient, if that's possible."

Hank entered the showroom asking loudly for her, and Derek swore again. "I need your undivided attention. I want to propose some ideas for broadening the yard's services."

"You sound serious."

"I am. Let's try it over dinner. No interruptions."

"Can't do dinner." She squeezed past him sideways, and the life jackets rubbed his chest.

"*Do* dinner? Nobody in Skerrystead *does* dinner."

"I can't *have* dinner with you. Previous engagement. Is that better?

"Marginally."

"Teak, I've got New York on hold."

"Coming," she called. "Derek, look, if it's really something we should talk over—"

He glanced at his watch. "Clear your decks here and come out to my shop. No phone. Lie to everybody if you have to. We can talk there."

She arched an eyebrow.

"What?" he muttered.

"Your suggestion contradicts the lecture you just gave me. What if one of my male employees should see me slipping into your shed, unescorted? I'd be alone, with a man of your reputation, right here in front of all these yard types."

"Give it up," he muttered.

"My sentiments exactly. I'll be there, but you're due for an earful from me, on topics we haven't even covered yet."

Teak left him in the aisle and headed for her office phone wishing that sparring with Derek Tate wasn't so invigorating, tantalizing and totally frustrating.

Her department vice president from Seavers and Cohn was on the line, which forced her to put all thoughts of the boatyard on hold. By the time she plowed through the business at hand, made arrangements for a trip to New York and got back to her employees and their requests, it was nearly five o'clock. Exhausted and still in need of a shower and makeover before her dinner date, she hustled to the shed, waving good-night to Manny as she went. Derek was bent over the *Kestral*.

"Sorry I'm late," she tried.

"I gave up on you."

"I said I'd be here, Derek."

"It's after five, how about rethinking dinner?"

"I'm having dinner with Brock."

"I thought as much. Is this going to become a habit?"

"My after-work habits are none of your concern. I hope you haven't fooled me into coming over here to give me another lecture on Brock Morrison, or any other personal topic, for that matter.''

''No.''

''It's only a dinner date.''

''I wanted to talk with you about lobstermen.''

''Skerrystead's commercial fleet?''

''Yes. I want to propose the idea of giving the commercial guys a place to work on their boats themselves, with access to the machine shop. I've been talking with Hank Maroney. He's—''

''You should have spoken with me first.'' Annoyance crept into her voice.

''It's a sound idea. He's not the only lobsterman who'd be willing to pay you rental fees if he could work on his own boats to keep his costs down. Let's put a meeting together. Have him pull in a few of the others who store their boats here.''

''A brainstorming session.''

''Right.''

''Under your direction?''

Derek wiped his hands on a rag. ''I'm thinking of the good of the yard, Teak. You're acting as if this is sabotage.''

''First you show up to store your boat. The next thing I know you're renting my shed and restoring my clients' boats. Now you're organizing a lobstermen's cooperative.''

"Don't get defensive, it's to bring in business. Just give me a chance to explain the details."

"It'll have to wait. I'm leaving for New York in the morning for a couple of days on Seavers and Cohn business."

He sighed. "New York, in the middle of this?"

"As I told you, it's part of the arrangement."

"Where do you stay?"

"On the couch of my apartment. Part of the arrangement when I sublet was being able to use my place when I need to come into town."

"Think it over while you're down there."

"I can't promise anything. I'm going down on business. As it is, I'll have more than enough to be thinking about."

At 9:45 that night Derek sat in his car and watched the headlights of Teak's truck wash the bogs as she skirted them and maneuvered her truck into her driveway. She got out, casting shadows as she passed through the beam of her outside lamp. He recognized the lamb's wool dress and put a fist to his ribs. She disappeared toward the back of the house. At 9:48 he inched his car onto the shoulder across the road and pulled the keys from his ignition.

He needed a reason for being there, but couldn't come up with anything clever. Instead, as he crossed the dark road, he imagined her look of surprise when she opened the door to find him on the stoop. His work boots crunched softly on the gravel drive as he followed her path along the side of the house.

"Good evening, Derek." The voice seemed to boom from the shadows.

"Damn!"

A self-satisfied Teak stood in the dark doorway. "Do you make it a habit to follow women home, or is this part of the *understanding* you told Brock we had?"

He winced under the sudden beam of the porch light and played with the keys in his hand as he strained for something logical to tell her. He could mention desire, need or infatuation. Passion came to mind. The fact that he was here at all was proof that the woman dissolved logic. That bit of information he'd keep to himself.

Impulsively he held out his key ring. "Forget the couch in your sublet apartment. I wanted to offer you our place. It's unoccupied this time of year. You'd be more comfortable."

"Our place?"

"My family keeps a co-op in the city. Dad and my brother are in and out on business and social events. I lived there briefly when I was with the company."

Teak flicked on a light and the kitchen behind her took on shape. She motioned for him to enter. As he stepped in, his shoulder brushed her sleeve and she caught her breath. His own pulse jumped.

"You make it hard to keep a train of thought," he muttered.

She smiled. "What if I hadn't come home? If I'd taken Brock up on his offer of a nightcap, would you be out at Breaker's Point right now, burrowed in his bushes?" The smile deepened to a laugh. "I can just imagine you emerging from Brock's shrubbery and offering me the key to your co-op." Her gaze softened. She stepped back against the cabinets, her hands out on either side of her on the countertop. "What's the real reason you've come out here?"

Derek shook his head slowly, all the while watching the expectation and warmth in her expression. "I could come up with another dozen excuses. The truth is..." He licked his lips and closed his eyes. Comprehension pumped a fresh dose of adrenaline through him. He could name the need, the ache. He could put shape and sound to it. He sucked in a breath and pulled back from the truth as if it had burned him. "You're good for my testosterone."

Her lashes lowered but her gaze stayed level. Expectation vanished as color spotted the hollow of her throat. Her breasts rose gently. She inhaled and smiled. "Simple chemistry," she murmured as she looked away, unfocused.

He knew the look, knew the strength that kept her on course. He was next to her in two strides but did nothing but put his hand over hers. "There was nobody but Hilary for a long, long time. There's been no one since."

She looked skeptical. "Why me?"

"Simple chemistry?"

"For which you have a simple solution."

She rotated her hand under his and pressed her fingers against his palm in a combination of innocence and sensuality. She was so close he felt her take a breath.

Derek pulled her into his arms where she stayed with her face against his chest. The pressure of her hands on his back moved over his spine. "Teak?"

"I'm beginning to think you might be right."

Derek moved his other hand. There were pillows and a bed and dim light from the kitchen. He kissed Teak's palm and wrist and ran his finger up her arm where the lamb's wool had been. The rush to begin was over. As if clock or conscience would break the spell, they had come to the room without a word, and hurried.

Teak had trembled as he unfastened the dress. It lay on the chair. His clothes were piled on the seat. There was no turning back. The familiar warmth of her lips teased his mouth as heat sank into sinew and bone. He welcomed her kiss and returned it, but his ache was for the unfamiliar.

The sound of his name was husky as he eased her onto the bed. Still kissing her, he opened his hands on her shoulders and slid his fingers down her back. She arched as he caressed her spine. "Just this one time. I've got to get you out of my system."

"Any reason can be the right one," he whispered. He played along the swell of her breast and began a trail of kisses over the softness and up along her jaw.

She reached for the packet on the bedside table and handed it to him, all the while working her own magic. He groaned and urged her on, mesmerized by his body's response. Every place she touched pulsated with desire as he repeated her name between urgent kisses.

Suddenly she cried out and buried her hands in his hair, urging him into her. He balanced above her and moved a pillow.

"We've fought this too long to hold back," she gasped.

"Don't hold anything back," he groaned.

"I couldn't."

Slowly he lowered himself. She trembled against him as she clung to his shoulders. Her breasts molded to his chest. Their shoulders touched. He shuddered. She was touching him, caressing, massaging, urging him into an ecstasy he'd fought for weeks. Suddenly heat and the intense ache for release plunged into him. Waves of desire seemed to roll out of her and into him, then back.

He followed her motion as it climbed through him once more. Suddenly a million physical sensations coalesced into the edge of ecstasy, thin, sharp as a knife blade. It swallowed him. He ground against her, chest to hips. She matched him. He pressed again. And again, weightless, mindless.

"Derek."

The sound was thick with desire. Suddenly she gripped his hips and held him, clung to him as tremors shook her. He pressed his face next to hers, filling himself with the sensation. "Come with me," she whispered, and it tore him open.

For long, sweet, unguarded moments Teak filled his hollowness. The rush of release was replaced by contentment as intense as any ecstasy.

When they were finally still, she touched his face. "I'll be gone when you wake up. That's the way I want it."

"I'll get up—"

"Promise me you won't," she whispered. "Let me go. I never would have done this if I hadn't known I could leave you behind in the morning. We got what we were after. Be satisfied with these moments and take them for what they were."

Teak's voice was thick. Derek would have guessed she was fighting tears, but there was no point in asking. The woman was a genius at denial.

Fifteen

Teak Brewster stood absolutely still and listened to the little voice inside her whispering that she was playing a very dangerous game. She was in the foyer of an understated, decidedly masculine environment. Dining room, living room and study fanned out from left to right in various combinations of taupe, leather, linen, first editions, original art and mahogany.

Her suitcase lay at the foot of a double bed in the second of three bedrooms roughly the size of her West Side apartment. She'd stashed a blueberry yogurt in the minimally stocked refrigerator of the spotless French blue kitchen and mistaken the empty maid's room off the breakfast area for the stairwell.

All of it could have passed for an architect's ranch design in an upscale suburban neighborhood except that Teak was fifteen floors above Park Avenue. New York hummed below her, almost muffling the pounding of her heart.

She was alone, but not without the feeling that one or another of the Tate family would appear at any moment and accuse her of breaking and entering. She dropped Derek's key into the ashtray on the table. She wished it were that easy to let go of his words, his touch, his *presence*.

Here in the cold light of mid-autumn, her behavior seemed unfathomable. It wasn't bad enough that she was finding it painful to let go of Skerrystead. In the course of a single month she'd fallen in love with a man who didn't have a clue about his own life and freely admitted tearing apart the life of the last woman who loved him.

And Teak knew how her own behavior would reflect on her at work. If Manny Souza got wind of what she had done, he'd chew her to pieces and use her for lobster bait. And she'd deserve it.

She walked to the nearest window and looked at the neighboring buildings. No romantic isolation here, no marsh grass, no calling gulls, no brooding cabinetmakers telling her more about herself than she wanted to hear.

This was the Big Apple, the source of her confidence, her sanity and her future. Resolutely she picked up the phone and dialed her office.

Her initial meeting at Seavers and Cohn went well. She reviewed the current accounts being overseen by her associates. However, the timetable they'd established was flawed. Two new accounts were demanding far more personal attention than anticipated. The department head gave her the news himself. They needed her back. There was more work than her associates could cover. As sympathetic as they were to her situation, her leave of absence had to be cut short. They needed her to return full-time by the first of December.

At four-thirty Teak took a cab to Park Avenue and picked up groceries at a corner market. She mulled over the situation as she fixed her dinner. Although she'd turned him down, a fellow with strong credentials named Jack Hammond had made the only bid on the boatyard. His offer had come over Labor Day and entailed his coming on as manager with an option to buy at some nebulous point in the future when a stronger economy would provide the needed financing.

She mulled it over. Bring in a manager with an option to buy. The only other solution was to close the yard, leaving Manny, Greg and her seasonal hands unemployed. Derek Tate would land on his feet. He always had. The others didn't have the luxury of trust funds and family houses to tide them over.

She massaged her temples against the rising headache and ate by herself in the living room. By the time night had fallen, she was no longer looking over her shoulder or jumping at the rattle of a pipe or squeak of a floorboard. She was engrossed in her business problems.

When she'd washed her few dishes, she showered and changed into her nightgown and robe, a silk set she'd treated herself to the winter before. She settled in the study with a stack of Seavers and Cohn files. She put a Lloyd-Weber CD in the player and poured herself a small brandy. As the music filled the room, she leaned back into the couch and opened the first file. Discipline. She stared at the sheaf of paper, the handwritten notes in the margin, the memos, the computer printouts.

Above the couch was a watercolor painting of Central Park in the snow. Next to her on the end table was a candid snapshot of two boys in a sailboat. She recognized the clubhouse of the Skerrystead Yacht Club. Brock Morrison came to mind and faded into Derek Tate. Derek in the boat shed, Derek in the Winsor Inn, Derek in her arms.

The music and the brandy began to work their melancholy magic. Tears squeezed between her lashes and slid over her cheeks. She looked at the watercolor. She looked at the snapshot. She whispered, "Damn you," and closed her eyes against the tears and the pain. Unfortunately, the liquor reminded her of their dinner at the Winsor Inn. The taste of it on her tongue was the taste of Derek. She could still feel the weight of him, the pressure of his body, the pain of leaving him asleep in her own house.

Something called to her from the surface of a dream. She blinked. The room was eerily still, the CD long finished. She opened her eyes. Derek Tate was sitting in the club chair diagonally across from her. He had on a chambray shirt and khaki pants, which she recognized. His socked feet were crossed on the coffee table in front of him. He was sipping the remains of her brandy. "Welcome back."

She cried out and sat up. "Derek! What are you doing here?"

Derek sat forward and put his feet on the floor. "I assumed you wouldn't be here."

"Ridiculous!"

"Obviously I saw the lights when I let myself in and found you like this."

Fully awake, Teak adjusted her robe and stood up. Shock and unwelcome pleasure were doing dangerous things underneath the silk, which seemed to cling in all the wrong places. She swiped at her cheeks. "And you sat in that chair staring at me!"

He stood. "I knew I'd scare the daylights out of you if I shook you awake so I thought—"

"You'd just sit there until I woke up?"

"It hasn't been long. In fact I've been sitting over there dreading this moment."

"Why have you done this after what I said last night, after what we decided?"

"*We* didn't decide a thing.

"Why are you here?"

"I doubt you'd believe me."

"Try me."

"I have some pieces in a shop on Madison Avenue. The gallery owner called this morning. A customer wants to meet me and talk over some designs."

"And that customer has to see you right now?"

"Yes. It's a couple and they're flying back to Santa Fe tomorrow afternoon."

"Preposterous. You should have let me know. I would have gone to my apartment."

Derek came to her. A gasp escaped from her throat, and he smiled. His hand grazed her arm as he reached and tapped a button on the telephone answering machine. Within seconds the sound of his voice and the full explanation were being spun back. Not only was there a full explanation, Derek's voice was sincere, apologetic and to the point.

A yawn worked its way through his chest, stretching the chambray over the shoulders and chest she'd so recently caressed. She felt the flush rise from her throat. Her breasts tingled as he washed her with a languid glance that coursed over every swell and curve. Desire betrayed her. She played with the robe. "I'm sorry," she managed. "I didn't think to check. If you'll call me a cab, I'll be out of here as soon as I change."

She was mildly surprised that he neither replied nor followed as she left the room, crossed the foyer and entered the bedroom where she'd left her belongings. She snapped on the bedside light and pulled her suitcase from the closet.

Derek let her go in the hopes that he could make sense of the need that had sunk its hooks into him so deeply. His laugh was sardonic. If he couldn't make sense of it last night, there sure as hell wouldn't be any clearheaded explanation enlightening him here.

Of course he hadn't taken his eyes off of her while she'd napped. Asleep, Teak had been an unnerving combination of relaxation, contentment and vulnerability he rarely saw when she was hauling boats or fussing with inventory. The challenge to hold onto that side of her played through him as incredible, erotic desire.

When he spoke again, he was leaning against the doorjamb of her room. "We have plenty of bedrooms. You don't need to flee across town."

She put the suitcase on the bed. "Central Park between us is a very good idea."

"Nothing between us is a better idea. Nothing but you and me and this big, empty bed." He was startled by tears welling in her eyes. "We're here. We're together. No employees to hide from, no pretense. Teak, make the most of this with me."

"I told you. Last night I got you out of my system."

"You don't believe that and neither do I."

"I do believe it. It's what I have to believe."

He crossed the room in his socks and fought the urge to pull her into his arms. Instead he sat on the edge of the bed in front of her. Under the silk her breasts rose and fell too rapidly. He shook his head slowly. "Tell me you don't want to make love to me again."

"What's the point in becoming involved in something that has to end?"

"Because I want to put my arms around you," he whispered as he stood up. As if she were glass he embraced her until her unconfined body reacted. She moaned.

He put his face to her temple. "Last night was incredible."

"I know," she murmured. "But it can't last. With our differences this will die a natural death. We don't have anything in common." The hollowness of her words raised a fear that threatened to strangle him. The realization of how he needed her was overwhelming.

"I don't want to let go of it yet," he replied. "The first of the year will be here before you know it and you'll be back here in New York on that fast track of yours. I'll be meeting deadlines in that boat shed. Enjoy the pleasure while you can." Shallow as they were, these words, this offer was as close to his own heart as he dared to look.

When she didn't resist, he touched her face. The suspense of the unknown had carried them the previous night. The known was a hundred times more powerful, and he knew she was as aware of it as he. He opened his fingers and slid the robe off her shoulders. With his thumb he played over the silk-covered tips of her breasts. She kissed him. The touch of her tongue was gentle, tentative, sweet. He gasped as her hands played over his buckle, belt, zipper. Fabric slid. Voices blended as he got out of his clothes.

She put her hands in his hair and pulled him to her breasts. The silk teased his overheated skin as one strap slid off her shoulder. His head filled with images of Teak as she'd been the night before, beneath him, needing him. He repeated her name. Her silk hem draped his wrist as he moved his hand to her thigh and up under the fabric. The overwhelming heat came again, bolting its way into him as she grabbed his wrist.

"Teak." The word was torn from his throat as he explored beneath the silk. She guided him with one hand and found him with the other. Her eyes were wide, dark, searching his as intimately as her hand was searching his body. The knife-edge of ecstasy ripped him open as he pulled her onto him and back onto the bed. He made love to her with the suitcase on one side and discarded clothing on the other.

Hours later Teak lay asleep, snuggled into his back. Her knees were tucked where his were, her breasts pressed against his spine so that he could feel her even breathing. It was the sedative he needed, and he began to doze.

Hours later, beneath the comforter, he awoke to the feel of her hand as she brushed his ribs. He was about to cover it with his own when she moved to his hip. He gasped softly as the intimacy grew. He felt her at his pelvic bone, over his thigh. Kisses teased the nape of his neck. He groaned and rhythm rose from him. He ground his hips against hers. She pressed forward, then back. His astonishment melded into an ache frighteningly deep.

''Teak,'' he groaned as he slammed his hips forward into her hand. She closed her fingers around him, tighter with each thrust, kissing his shoulders, his spine. Lost in her touch, aroused beyond anything he'd ever known, he moved to his back. He brought her roughly onto him and pulled her down, finally returning the kisses and caresses. He tried to concentrate on her pleasure as release came, but Teak Brewster's magic had taken him so deeply into himself it was impossible.

For a long time he lay on his side staring into the dark room. Few things in life scared Derek Tate. The depth of his contentment and the need for its source were two.

Sixteen

After breakfast they kissed goodbye. Teak went off to her office, Derek to his client. At eleven, as she'd arranged, Teak called the Madison Avenue address he'd given her, to tell him she'd finished with Seavers and Cohn. By noon she was tipping her cabdriver and crossing the sidewalk to the Keyser Gallery. The showroom was intimate and exquisitely tasteful.

Teak was no stranger to the upscale neighborhood shops and world-famous stores that surrounded the Keyser Gallery. Excitement swelled in her as she entered and spotted Derek in the corner.

He and the gallery director were standing in front of his Newport block-front chest, which even to the trained eye could have passed for a priceless antique. Next to it were the matched set of contemporary chairs she recognized from his portfolio, as close to sculpture as seats. The contrast, the man and the possibilities made her smile.

Her heart fluttered as Derek looked up, grinned and crossed the exhibit area. "The Keysers want to give me a one-man show as soon as I can build up my stock, most likely in the spring."

She hugged him. "Congratulations!"

"There's more. John and Maureen Butler, the couple from Santa Fe, are flying me out the first of December to look over their spread, as they call it. Get a feel for their taste so I can design some things."

"Some things?"

"A desk for him with matching bookcases and a boardroom table, all for his office. Maybe a dining table for the house. I can't wait to get back to the boat shed and my drafting table."

Teak ignored the twinge at the mention of Skerrystead. "Lunch first?"

He kissed her ear. "Your choice. Why don't we walk someplace. Something close to the park?"

Although the November air was brisk, there was little wind. The mood and Derek were enough to keep Teak warm as they meandered up Madison

Avenue and found a fashionable restaurant with less than a twenty-minute wait. "I eat here on weekends," Teak said as their orders were placed in front of them. "The salads are fabulous. Their fish is fresh."

"Nothing beats Skerrystead Fish Market."

"Skerrystead. Let's concentrate on where we are."

"I still want to tell you about my proposal for the commercial fishermen."

"I know, and I'll listen, but not right now. That life melts away when I'm here."

Derek was quiet. "I've hardly thought of anything else." When she looked at him he grinned. "Except making love to you."

His eyes shone, and his expression exuded confidence. Over lunch he talked about his relationship with his father and the approaching Thanksgiving holiday. "My mother'll be with her side of the family out on the coast, but my brother and his wife use the apartment. They treat the kids to a show, the museums. Dad will probably be here, too."

"Then you should be. It's the perfect chance to tell him about Santa Fe and the Keyser show. From what I know of Judson Tate, he needs tangible proof of success. You've got plenty, Derek. Thanksgiving was made for fence-mending."

Derek continued to talk about his work as they left the restaurant. They considered a visit to the Metropolitan Museum of Art, since it was just up Fifth Avenue, but opted instead for a cab and the galleries of Greenwich Village and SoHo. Teak swung her arm through his as they started at Washington Square and worked their way down MacDougal Street.

"How could you give this up? New York is bursting with creativity."

"I can't think of a place that stifles it faster."

"But the Keyser, your Santa Fe connection—"

"I have no qualms about exhibiting here, or coming up to meet clients. It's the hassles of getting anything accomplished, the pressure, the stress—"

"Down here you could have a workshop and loft in the same space. From what I saw of your setup in Wellfleet, that would suit you fine."

He hunched his shoulders against the cold. "The boatyard suits me fine. You know what it took to get where I am."

"This won't ever be home again?"

Derek shook his head. "Skerrystead is home."

The twinge grew painful. "Home is where the heart is."

"And yours, Teak? Maybe now's the time to talk about it."

"Before you have another Hilary on your hands?"

"Since you brought it up, yes. I broke our engagement because she was miserable, horrified by what I wanted to do with my life. As painful as it was, even she would tell you that calling it quits was the right thing. Once I left Tate and she realized she couldn't talk me into going back, we had no future together." He stopped suddenly and let half a dozen people hustle past. The afternoon light brightened his eyes, but there was no humor in them. "Is history repeating itself?"

She hesitated. "There's no point in discussing my heart. Seavers and Cohn want me back here by December first."

"So we skip to the punch line before you even tell the joke."

"This is no joke. This is my life, damn it. *My* life. I've worked unbelievably hard to get where I am with the firm. I worked even harder to get out of Skerrystead, to put all of that behind me. You know good and well that I came back to the yard because Pop's death left me no choice. I had Manny and Greg and the others to think of."

"Seems to me you came back once for someone you loved."

"It's not the same thing as this situation."

"That was love that shaped your past, Teak."

"And what I feel for you is love enough to shape my future? I mean, what do you feel for me?"

"Something that overwhelms me. Something that makes me feel connected, to you, to my work..." He paused. "And if I really, truly loved you I'd make a permanent commitment to the yard? Is that where this conversation is going? We've been so busy rolling around in the sheets, the subject hasn't even come up."

Derek began to walk. "December first is a month ahead of your schedule. Who'll replace you?"

"I had a few offers before I decided to run it myself. Jack Hammond from Hyannis wanted to come on as manager with an option to buy."

"If it had been a decent offer, he'd be there already."

"The financing didn't work."

"What about your apartment here? There's a Julliard student in it."

"Stop pressing. I just got the word yesterday. It may take some time to put things in place. I'll manage. I always have."

"With the world at arm's length. *Managing* is a lousy substitute for living life. I know. I did it for years."

"My life can't begin to compare to yours, in any category."

"Thank God."

She glanced at her watch. "I've got to go back and pack. I think it's best if I take an evening shuttle."

"You were supposed to stay another night."

"As I've said, things changed at the office. The sooner I get back and—"

He took her hand. "The things I said last night were all I could bring myself to recognize. I love you, Teak. *Connected* is the best way for me to describe what I feel when I'm with you, part of something bigger than myself, part of a whole. We have more in common than you think, and I'd like to believe we have a future together."

"In Skerrystead."

"Yes. You're running away from yourself, and that's damned hard to do."

Her eyes were wide, serious and at the same time guarded. "Let me guess. You did it for years."

"Are you going to stand there and tell me you can walk away from what we've shared this last week?"

"You did it for years," she repeated. Teak turned his hand over in hers and brushed his palm with her fingers. The now-familiar gesture was as bittersweet as it was sensual.

"Derek, I've known you all your life. I know the kind of kid you were, the kind of teenager, the kind of man, the kind of fiancé. You haven't stuck with anything or anyone long enough to let real love develop. Infatuation's as far as you've gotten, and that's where you are with me. It's incredibly flattering, but even if I liked the idea of staying at the boatyard, I'd have to be a fool to sacrifice Wall Street and all I've worked for on the chance that what you feel is more than a whim."

"Can you tell me you don't love me?"

"I do love you. That's the awful part. That's also why I'm getting on that plane. One more night in your arms and I'd start to believe in this fantasy. I was crazy to make love to you the first time. Last night was pure lunacy."

"That's not how I would describe it," he whispered.

She flushed. "I want to get a cab. Please stay and finish the galleries."

Derek pressed his fist against the pain in his chest. Teak, don't do this. Don't run away again."

"It's the way I cope. I need to. Facing you at the boatyard for the next week will be hard enough. Please give me time to go back to the apartment and pack, by myself. I want to be gone when you get back."

Seventeen

November in Skerrystead, even under optimum conditions, was apt to be gray, biting, bitter and wet, a perfect reflection of Teak's disposition as she returned to the boatyard to concentrate on the tangle of business that lay ahead of her. She got in touch with Jack Hammond. For all his enthusiasm, he was no closer to meeting her price for the yard than he had been the first time, and he couldn't start as manager until after New Year's.

Teak considered her options. She could put Manny in charge in the interim, give the entire staff an extended unpaid vacation and close the yard

during December—or wait for her fairy godmother to swoop down and wave her magic wand.

Melissa DiReste, the Julliard student subletting
her apartment, was disgustingly cheerful about
doubling up, would be gone for the Christmas holidays anyway, and would sleep on the couch. She
also asked how Teak felt about the trombone and
mentioned her boyfriend and his jazz band who
dropped by occasionally after a gig.

Derek returned two days after Teak. That is, his
car appeared in front of his boat shed. He stayed in
his workshop, and she stayed out of it. For the rest
of the week his car was the only indication that the
man was on the premises. Glancing at it made her
heart ache, but she found business life bearable
once she realized that he intended to spend his entire workday in the corrugated building.

Her third day back she sipped coffee and spun in
her office chair until she could see his bumper
through her window. How could she have possibly
thought that a night in the man's arms would purge
her heart of what she felt for him? How could she
possibly have thought their second night together
would be anything she could walk away from?

It seemed an eternity since she'd been so naive.
She loved him. She'd told him she loved him, but
there was no fairy godmother to wave away the reality that sacrifice would have to be part of that
love.

The weekend came and went. Monday morning she was late arriving and when she entered her office, Derek Tate swiveled around in her chair and got to his feet. It was discouraging that he looked as robust and handsome as ever.

"Morning, Teak."

"This is a surprise."

"You know me. I can't stay away."

Their glances held. "Coffee?"

"Had some." He crossed the room. "The work on *Kestral*'s finished. You might want to let the Bendettes know. They'll want to come down and look things over before they pay for my repair."

"All right."

"As it turns out, I'm leaving for Santa Fe tonight."

Her eyes burned. "Earlier than expected."

"Getting out of here ahead of time suits my schedule. I've taken your suggestion about spending Thanksgiving with my father. I'll fly from Santa Fe directly to New York and see him there."

"I hope it does you both good."

"Thanks."

The stilted conversation swung between them with the weight of a clock pendulum. As he started for the door, Teak put up her hand. "What are the chances that Santa Fe might turn out to be something big?"

"More offers?"

"Yes. Once you're introduced, you make connections with designers and architects and they see your furniture. I know how these things work."

"There's a possibility."

"Then you should consider it. If you need to relocate, I won't hold you to the promise to stay here."

"Another change of heart?"

"Nothing's changed in my heart. It's just that my plans have been rearranged. Under the circumstances it doesn't seem fair to hold you to that promise to stay with the yard."

"Does Seavers and Cohn have a branch office in New Mexico?"

"No."

"If it did, would you come out there? Yes or no."

"Derek, this has nothing to do with me."

"Teak, darling, this has everything to do with you. You're still calling the shots. First you wanted me to stay here. Now that we're—" he looked out the window "—whatever the hell it is that we are to each other, you want me to follow you back to New York. I've said no to that, and now comes the subtle suggestion that I put the American continent between us."

"I was only thinking of you."

He came to her. "Night and day? Here in this office and home in that bed were we first made love? Do you ache, Teak, the way I do? Do you want to shake sense into me, force me to mold myself to fit your life so it can be *our* life? That sure as hell is what I want.''

''Derek, don't.''

''Believe me, I hate this. I want to sleep. I want to eat and work and design without constantly thinking of you. I want to get rid of that horrible feeling of hope that's kept me going since I first laid eyes on you.''

''So do I,'' she cried, swiping at tears.

''For now, Santa Fe is my answer. After that I can concentrate on the holidays with my family. I figure by the time I get back here, it'll be December. You'll be gone. Maybe I'll be cured.'' He opened the door to the showroom. ''Good luck on Wall Street. I really mean that. You'll be CEO before you know it.''

Teak sank into her chair. The moment she heard him close the door as he left, she sank her forehead onto the desk and pressed her fists against her eyes.

December third was a Monday. Snow flurries drifted past the Tate Park Avenue window in sharp contrast to the weather Derek had left behind in Santa Fe. With the exception of himself, the apartment was empty. He was back in the armchair, feet on the coffee table. The Lloyd-Weber CD was playing again. No one, however, lay curled in fitful sleep on the couch.

He was living on the remnants of turkey and cranberry sauce and, as the last to depart, had promised his father and brother he'd leave the kitchen free of leftovers that would spoil.

December third. First day back. "It must be love," he muttered as he wrapped himself in his parka, had the doorman hail him a cab. He gave the driver Teak's West Side address. No phone calls. No postcards from the Southwest had been sent. None from Cape Cod or Manhattan had been received. There'd been no communication between them, and it ate at him like an ulcer.

He paid his fare and entered her building, gave his name and Teak's to the doorman who announced his arrival on the intercom and sent him to the elevators, with a brisk, "Five C."

He got off the elevator and pulled a lease from his pocket as he buzzed the apartment.

"You're here to see Teak?" The voice came from behind the door.

"Yes."

A twenty-year-old blonde opened the door. Behind her, at a small dining table, a fellow about her age was eating spaghetti.

"Hey, come on in. I'm Melissa DiReste." She motioned behind her. "This is Justin Turnbridge, New York's best trombonist."

"I was looking for Teak."

"Right. That's why I had you buzzed on up. She's not due for a few more weeks."

"Not December first?"

"Couldn't work out the boatyard business. Lucky for me, huh? I would have been on the couch."

"But she is coming back?"

"Oh, sure."

"I thought her office— Never mind. Tell her I came by if you talk to her." He tripped over the trombone case on the way out and swore to himself all the way across town. He'd missed nearly a week of work, let clients slide, *stayed in New York* just to surprise her. Now who was being naive?

He spent the evening cleaning out the refrigerator and the morning on the shuttle to Hyannis. His car sat in the lot where he'd left it, covered with frost. It was about the same reaction he expected when he reached the boatyard.

Eighteen

Teak was in shed four looking at the engine of the yacht club launch with Manny when the sound of a familiar car engine made her raise her head. It stopped outside.

"He's back," Manny said as he got to work. "I was you, I'd lay one of those responsibility lectures on him you're so good at." He arched a single brow. "'Course, I ain't you."

She smiled. "Thanks for the advice. I do need to tell him about the Bendettes." Despite her attempts to quell the butterflies, her stomach flip-flopped as she pulled on her jacket and walked into the midmorning air.

Derek had already slammed the door and was heading toward his workshop. She called him and watched the breeze play in his hair as he waited for her. She tried desperately to read his expression, but found nothing in it but anticipation.

"Hello," she tried. Her breath came in soft gray puffs.

"Hello."

"You're timing couldn't be better. The Bendettes are coming down this afternoon. I was hoping you'd be here. I left a message on your tape this morning, in case you were still at your apartment. Is that where you've been?"

"Yes, but I didn't get the message. I must have already left."

"How was Santa Fe?"

"Productive."

She waited and finally said, "They liked you?"

"Yes. I have quite a project lined up. We went over the preliminaries before I flew to New York. That's where I've been."

"You stayed quite a while longer than you said you would. Were you patching things up with your father?"

"Some." He stuffed his hands into his pockets. "I'm in desperate need of some coffee."

"Follow me."

"And some more conversation. Go fill two mugs and bring them back out here." He squinted at the sky. "Please."

Five minutes later they were sitting on the pier, backs against the pilings. Geese honked. Teak watched them circle and settle in their V formation. "There's a bunch of Canada geese that never migrate anymore."

"They live out on the meadows at the point."

"They must get enough food or their radar's all confused, or something."

"Maybe they like it enough to stay in Skerrystead."

"Maybe."

"Teak—"

She said, "Derek," at the same time and they laughed weakly.

"I didn't come out here to talk about geese. I thought you were due back on Wall Street this week. I stayed in New York to see you. Instead I met Melissa and a trombone player."

"You went to my apartment?"

He fished in his chest pocket. "I had a whole lecture planned."

"I have one, too."

"You might start by explaining what you're doing here."

"Manny would tell you that I'm here because the fellow with the offer, Jack Hammond, can't do anything for me until after New Year's. When I told Seavers and Cohn I couldn't change our original agreement, I expected to get fired or at the very least demoted.''

''You're here so I'll assume you're indispensable, irreplaceable.''

''They shuffled me to another department.''

''Compromise?''

''Yes.'' His expression made her smile. ''I've been thinking about that very word. A lot.''

''Care to explain what you meant by 'Manny would tell you'?''

''There's another reason I'm still here. The idea of loving you scares me to death.'' She buried her thoughts in another sip of coffee.

''But the alternatives are about as appealing as cold coffee grounds?''

''I thought, since I had the opportunity to be here a few more weeks, we might try and make sense of what's going on. Will you be going back to Santa Fe?''

''Occasionally.''

''Not permanently?''

''No boats to repair.''

Derek grinned, sipped, closed his eyes and put his face up to the cold air. ''Smell the sea?''

''Yes.''

He handed her the folded contract and waited as she opened it. When she realized what she was reading, she raised her head slowly. "This is a lease for something on Spring Street."

"SoHo."

"I don't understand."

"I didn't either. Not for days, weeks. Not until I got far enough away to clear the fog. I love you, Teak. I want you in my bed, in my arms, in my life. If I can't have it any other way, then it'll be New York."

"You'd give up Skerrystead?"

"It's the last resort of a desperate man. I planned to rent a loft long enough to find my own answers. It was either that or set up my saws and tools in my old man's library. Park Avenue doesn't take kindly to sawdust."

"You'd have done that for me?"

"I could ask the same of you."

"The answer would be yes."

"You'll consider staying here, not selling?"

"Long before you walked into this yard I was having trouble with the yearning I feel for this place. I don't want to love it."

"How well I know. But you do, Teak."

"It's as much a part of me as the Tate boys and the sand hills and the Souzas and Harbor Street."

"That's not so bad."

"I can't let go of it, any more than I can let go of you."

He kissed her with the gulls cawing and the wind whistling between the sheds. "I'm here. You're here. We've got the time to work this out and the perfect place to do it."

"Scary business," she murmured.

"It's not so bad when somebody you love's right there with you, every step of the way."

The geese were nothing but a distant V as they headed for the nearest bog. They'd be back. "And look where it's brought me!"

"Full circle. Out into the world and back into the life of somebody who needs you."

"Pop would think he failed me."

"Bud Brewster would know he'd raised his youngest to follow her heart," was all Derek could manage before he kissed her.

*   *   *   *   *

SILHOUETTE® Desire®

MAN OF THE MONTH: 1993

They're tough, they're sexy...
and they know how to get the
job done....
Caution: They're

MEN AT WORK

Blue collar... white collar... these men are working overtime
to earn your love.

July:	Undercover agent Zeke Daniels in Annette Broadrick's ZEKE
August:	Aircraft executive Steven Ryker in Diana Palmer's NIGHT OF LOVE
September:	Entrepreneur Joshua Cameron in Ann Major's WILD HONEY
October:	Cowboy Jake Tallman in Cait London's THE SEDUCTION OF JAKE TALLMAN
November:	Rancher Tweed Brown in Lass Small's TWEED
December:	Engineer Mac McLachlan in BJ James's ANOTHER TIME, ANOTHER PLACE

Let these men make a direct deposit into your heart.
MEN AT WORK... only from Silhouette Desire!

MOM93JD

Relive the romance...
Harlequin and Silhouette
are proud to present

by Request

A program of collections of three complete novels by the most requested authors with the most requested themes. Be sure to look for one volume each month with three complete novels by top name authors.

In June: **NINE MONTHS** Penny Jordan
Stella Cameron
Janice Kaiser

Three women pregnant and alone. But a lot can happen in nine months!

In July: **DADDY'S HOME** Kristin James
Naomi Horton
Mary Lynn Baxter

Daddy's Home ... and his presence is long overdue!

In August: **FORGOTTEN PAST** Barbara Kaye
Pamela Browning
Nancy Martin

Do you dare to create a future if you've forgotten the past?

Available at your favorite retail outlet.

SILHOUETTE® Desire®

RED, WHITE AND BLUE...
Six sexy, hardworking, hometown hunks who were
born and bred in the USA!

NEED PROTECTION?
Then you must read ZEKE #793 by Annette Broadrick
July's Man of the Month

NEED TO TAKE THE PLUNGE?
Then dive into BEN #794 by Karen Leabo

NEED TO GET AWAY?
Then sail away with DEREK #795 by Leslie Davis Guccione

NEED TO FIND YOUR ROOTS?
Then dig into CAMERON #796 by Beverly Barton

NEED A MAN?
Then warm up with JAKE #797 by Helen R. Myers

NEED A HAND?
Then you need to meet WILL #798 by Kelly Jamison

Desire invites you to meet these sexy, down-home guys! These hunks
are HOT and will make you pledge allegiance to the all-American man!

SDRWB